Flânerie*

will get you Nowhere

Written by
SANDY WOOLWORTH

Illustrations by
CAROL TIPPIT WOOLWORTH

* **flânerie** |flän(ə)ˈrē|
noun
aimless idle behavior.

ORIGIN
French, from *flâner* and *flaneur* 'saunter, lounge.'

TipWorth Press ISBN: 978-0-9852645-4-3

for ebook: 978-0-9852645-5-0

This book,

and the series to which it belongs,

would only be half complete

if it were not for the

beautiful design and layout

along with the illustrations

conceived and drawn

by my wife,

Carol Tippit Woolworth.

For Dora

An Idea

Marie-Christine sat down at the kitchen table after completing her five morning activities, the same five she always completed before she started work.

Number one: boil water and prepare the coffee.

Number two: feed Evelyn, her cat, and Schnitzel, her dog.

Number three: get a croissant from the counter, and butter from the refrigerator, to eat along with the coffee.

Number four: smoke her one and only cigarette of the day, which leads finally to number five.

Number five, which was to be a turning point in Marie-Christine's life, not to mention the lives of others,

Number five: read the morning newspaper.

Marie-Christine sat down at the kitchen table. All activities were completed excepting one, reading the morning newspaper. She had gotten through the serious stuff like the politics, the crime, and the pleasant things like the general comings and goings of people in Paris and France in general, and was working her way to her favorite part of the paper: culture, which included entertainment news plus movie and TV listings.

Marie-Christine sat down at the kitchen table. She had thought a lot about sitting. About how much time she spent sitting in a day, a week, a year, a lifetime. Sitting, and her routine. Get up at 5am. Make the bed. Go to the bathroom. Go to the front door for the paper. Do the five activities. Shower. Dress. Walk two blocks to the garage to get her cab. Go to the airport. Sit and drive and talk or not talk. Break for lunch; a baguette, some cheese, an apple, an Orangina. Sit and drive. Wait. Talk to the other drivers she has waited with and spoken to for so many years. Worry when not talking. Worry about bills, worry about her two nephews who have borrowed money from the American, worry about what the future held for a 50 year old woman in a crumbling France. Then she read the headline below:

LE GRAND JOURNAL
8-9 PM WEDNESDAY
AUTHOR REYNALDO DUMONT
AND HIS WIFE, ARTIST FRANCINE DUMONT
WITH THEIR CORGI, WINNIE,
WILL DISCUSS THE SECOND ADVENTURE IN
THEIR BOOK SERIES "THE WINNIE CHRONICLES"
ENTITLED "THE DOGPYRE SYNDROME"

Marie-Christine stumbled to her feet. She had an idea. Just the germ of an idea, but as the pieces came together, it became a very doable idea. She reached for the phone to call Gilles and Laurent and hoped Laurent would answer since he was the smarter of the two. The really smart one. Gilles wasn't dumb, but rather too much like herself: routine oriented, average; uneducated. Laurent had a law degree and big ideas. Laurent and his big ideas. One of the reasons they were in trouble with the American was because Laurent had big ideas.

The brothers Boucher lived together in a three-room apartment. They were in their early thirties and looked the part of the cool, young, Parisian male. They were also about to lose their apartment, and Paris and have to "go on the run" from their "creditor" in a week, maybe two weeks, but definitely soon.

Marie-Christine knew all about it. Laurent even asked if she would like to be a part of it. It was simple and fool proof and dangerous because it involved importing drugs. Laurent would provide the "capital," and used the word capital instead of money or euros. "Capital," he said, thinking that made it all very business like and respectable.

"The only capital required of you would be 20,000 euros," Laurent said, as if that was the easiest thing in the world to do. "I can borrow the rest from Dad's

American friend." My brother had a few American friends. They broke your legs if you didn't pay them what you owed them. They were bad news and so was this crazy idea of Laurent's. Poor Gilles was involved, too. And, wouldn't you know, it wasn't so foolproof after all. The supplier of the drugs dropped dead of a heart attack while transporting four kilos of cocaine, which were then impounded by the police. One of those kilos impounded kilos belonged to Laurent and Gilles and now they had no way to pay back the American.

"Laurent, get over here now. We have to talk." Marie-Christine said. And the rest was history.

Gone Fishing

I awoke with arthritis pain in my hips, preventing the enjoyment of a deep dream. Even my three-times-a-day baby aspirin couldn't stave off the waves of pain. An aspirin a day kept the Dogpyre away, but arthritis seemed to be a tougher foe.

I raised my head off the floor and took in the night. From behind my bed of towels and blankets that I regularly slept with, I saw that Francine was awake too. She had rigged a book light to her drawing pad and was sketching. The reflection of the light from the pad onto her forehead highlighting the deep indentation on the right side, reminded me of the head trauma she'd suffered some time ago when we all participated in a plane crash. Shocking, I know, but also ancient history. From that dark time how far we had come.

Francine saw me looking. Her features went up and her teeth reflected the light, making me aware of how happy she was to see me awake. Placing her drawing pad on Reynaldo, who was in oblivion, she swung her legs out from under the covers and crawled over to me.

I was anticipating something good happening, such as a midnight snack, which was silly, or perhaps a snuggle with Francine in the moonlight.

Well, surprise! Not a snuggle, but a full-fledged lift-me-up, on to her shoulder and out the bedroom door, down the hall to the stairs leading to the kitchen. Several things registered in equal parts as she hoisted my half-limp body to her chest and shoulder. One, ouch, my hips were killing me. Par for the course, so I paid it little mind. Two, breakfast! This was a pain stopper. Food trumps pain every time and this posture, this route and the high pitched cooing along with the word breakfast spoken in a squeaky fashion could have meant only one thing. Food. The focus was on food so the pain stayed in the bedroom. On my way down I heard the alarm clock in the bedroom go off provoking a groan from Reynaldo.

In the kitchen I was gently placed on the floor in front of the sink as the morning coffee was prepared. Reynaldo appeared and they did their morning kiss and hug, and I gave them a morning bark to signal my disapproval of such behavior, causing a laugh and a pat on my head.

It was still dark out but the morning routine had begun, way too early if you'd asked me, and this was a clue that something was up. Anytime there was a deviation from our 5:20 AM wakeup time, I would wager that something was up. I didn't have the facility to guess what it might be, but it did instill a little anxiety.

But not enough anxiety to forgo what had just appeared in my bowl. Did I say anxiety? I'm sure I meant hunger. The offering was broiled chicken with barley, carrots, green beans, millet, rice, peas with buttermilk on top. It tasted so good and I could never figure out why Reynaldo and Francine weren't down there with me eating out of my bowl. I'd let them. I think it would be fun, but it had never occurred to them to do this.

I looked up at the windows and saw that the light was changing. There were suspicious noises being made somewhere in the house. A clue to future events was the sound of suitcases being brought up from the basement. This meant travel. Possibly air travel, which always meant that I'd go into a crate placed in a dark, cold, and scary part of the airplane, away from everyone, along with some other sad animals, helpless and alone.

A few hours worth of time had transpired from the sound of

the suitcases to now — hours filled with car loading, car travel, and general airport hubbub. And so, I was correct about my prediction of travel. And I was half right about the airplane too. We were now definitely in an airplane except this time I was on a seat, a big leather seat with a blanket and a pillow. A lady brought me treats and I had a bowl of water on the floor. Francine was right next to me and Reynaldo was across the aisle in a seat exactly like mine.

Lots of other people were also there, walking in the aisle, sitting like Francine and Reynaldo, talking, sleeping while sitting up, or drinking things. The lady who brought the treats petted me a lot and spoke to Francine and Reynaldo all of the time.

At one point, after a really nice nap, Francine put a bowl of food directly in front of my snout. It wasn't chicken or ground beef; it was, and I only know this because I overheard Francine say this to the lady, fish. Fish! I've never heard of it. I ate it, of course, but never to my knowledge, had I ever eaten fish.

As I contemplated the fish in my bowl, the first thing that hit me was the smell. This was to be expected as smelling is the name of the game here. But this smell was talking to me. It was saying "Don't you remember me? Don't you remember your swim in the ocean? The long, cold, lonely nights drifting in the Atlantic with no food or water?" That's what the smell was, the smell of the ocean triggering these memories. Well, maybe not memories. More like unpleasant impulses that Dogspeak had translated into something like memories. Was this off putting? I can't really say because I'm a dog and what I was faced with was a bowl full of food and I was drooling, which meant that I was beyond any control over my next action.

Chomp. OK! Mushy texture, easy on the tongue. No tooth work at all. This was a tongue food pure and simple. I've done tongue work before when I was given a total rice meal for a stomach disorder, so I could easily handle fish. And I would imagine you know by now that flavor didn't always enter into the picture when I ate. Yes, yes, when Francine cooked my ground beef or chicken meal, I did savor it. I'd let the flavor register in that nano-second I allowed her food to stay in my mouth before I swallowed. But in this bowl, with fish being something new and not from Francine, I mashed with my tongue and then instantly swallowed. No taste registered. Was there an after-taste? I was trying to find one but with all that goes on in my mouth between the incredibly strong enzymes in my saliva and the ancient food residue in my aging teeth, there's invariably an after-taste, and unfailingly, an "aura" around my mouth. I've always found it to be pleasant. Others? Well lets just say the jury is out on that.

I do have to say that the fish was good. Our routine dictated that after dinner a walk would be required. I didn't know this, but Francine was not planning to take me for a walk. We were all in this tubular room with the rushing sound and no one was leaving.

OK, I was able to deal with this. I, as a dog, put up with everything so why not this. And, frankly, the portion was on the small side. In times past I've eaten an entire bag of dog food. So I wasn't concerned. But after dinner we'd always go for a walk, or roll, in my wheelchair, so not going seemed a little strange. I was at their mercy, and I accepted the no walk circumstance. I realized that the best thing to do was sleep. And just when I came to that conclusion, the lights dimmed and things got quiet and cozy and before I knew it people were snoring, which told me sleep was happening all over the place.

Sleep, an activity I have always loved almost as much as I've loved food, came easily to me. I would guess that I slept most of the time, maybe as much as 23 hours a day. In this atmosphere, with the darkness and the constant rushing sound, there was absolutely no effort involved. I closed my eyes, one at a time, and drifted away dreaming of the ocean.

Is This Off the Meter?

We landed safely and left the plane with much goodwill among our fellow passengers and stewards. I was so popular that I received several pettings on the way out. Once we were in the terminal Francine put me into my wheels, freeing up Reynaldo for an extra bag. After customs we headed for GROUND TRANSPORTATION to get a taxi. The queue for taxis was quite long, but for some reason, we were taken ahead of the others. A nondescript man motioned for us to follow him to what turned out to be a black, late model Mercedes. He wore a hooded sweatshirt, baseball cap pulled low to his sunglasses, and dark baggy trousers and didn't seem to be part of the well-organized taxi line. Reynaldo, though a little skeptical, decided to go with him because we were to meet our friend Paulette at the hotel very shortly, and waiting in the queue would have made us late.

He was nice enough, placed our bags in the trunk, opened the taxi doors for us, but didn't utter a word, even when Reynaldo tipped him. Our driver was a pleasant women in her fifties. Next to her was a large bag of groceries blocking her name and the meter on the dashboard.

"Bonjour, Mademoiselle. Thanks for taking us ahead of the others. You must know the taxi guy the way he motioned for you," Reynaldo said as he settled into the back seat and closed the door.

"Non, Monsieur. That was just a lucky chance for me," Marie-Christine said as she pulled out of the taxi line.

"What a life saver, but he shouldn't have moved us ahead of the line like that. We would have managed if we had to wait our turn," Francine said as she put me on the back seat between Reynaldo and her.

"I think he fell in love with your dog," said Marie-Christine. "Where can I take you?"

"Oh yes, she's definitely a charmer," Reynaldo was scrolling his iPhone for the address. "We're going to number 1 Place Vendôme, s'il vous plait." He then called Paulette Espin, and told her they were on their way and should be there in about forty minutes.

"Oui, Monsieur. Hotel De Vendôme. You will be staying long in Paris?" asked Marie- Christine. She was maneuvering through the Parisian traffic quite speedily, causing me to slide uncomfortably close to the edge of the seat.

"Just a short while," Francine said as she placed me on the floor for some much needed stability. And then to Reynaldo, "Does Paulette know where our hotel is?"

"She's staying nearby. She said she's already seen our hotel on a walk she took this morning," replied Reynaldo.

"I too have un chien. Usually here next to me, but he is sick today. You have traveled with your dog before?" asked Marie-Christine.

"Uh huh. One time, to England," said Reynaldo as he patted my head.

"I see, a world traveler. Did she travel well?" asked Marie

Christine.

"Well, sadly, no, she was involved in a dreadful accident," said Reynaldo.

"Our plane crashed in the Atlantic," Francine added.

"Ah, oui. But of course. Then she must be Winnie! Am I correct, Madam?"

"So you've heard of her," said Francine, trying to find the clasp for her seatbelt.

"Oui, of course, Madam. I've heard of all of you. Was she afraid to fly again? Her ordeal was such a sensation over here, in the papers and TV for weeks, and then the recent animation. Everyone went to see it!"

"She was a bit frightened at first, but settled in O.K. She flew in the cabin with us, so it was nice for her," said Francine who was still having trouble with her seat belt.

"They let her fly in the cabin? She is more of a celebrity than I thought. But of course, pourquoi pas? I remember the news stories about her ocean swim and meeting the Queen. Oceandog. This is what they called her, non? The airline was happy to have her, n'est-ce pas? I read that she will appear on television this week."

"On *Le Grand Journal*," Said Reynaldo.

"Oui, oui, oui, very popular show. I usually watch it. I imagine Winnie must make a lot of money! Forgive me, I didn't mean to say that, but to think, the animation, books, Dogspeak. She is quite a commodity, non? And then she was also part of the Dogpyre phenomenon. What a life story she has!" exclaimed Marie-Christine.

"She does have quite a history," replied Francine, smiling down at me after giving Reynaldo a perplexed look out of the corner of her eye.

"Excusez moi, I must take this call," said Marie Christine over the ring tone "An der schonen blauen Donau (The Blue Danube Waltz)," coming from her phone. She whispered in French, I couldn't hear all of the words, but some came through. All in French, but faithfully translated by Dogspeak. She said my name, and I heard both Francine's and Reynaldo's names mentioned.

I then heard, "everything is O.K. here. Have you set up the rooms?" And, "Non, they haven't had a chance to see my face, I did the rearview mirror, and am in my wig as we discussed. Don't worry about me," and "What do you mean pistolet (the gun)?" then something about "rue Chaptal,"

It was during this interlude that I saw something on the floor and tried to get to it — a piece of candy — causing Francine to reprimand me. As much as I wanted that hard and dirty morsel, I also reveled in Francine's effort to retrieve it from my mouth. (I love how her fingers feel when they go in my mouth, wiggling in their search for whatever ill-gotten contraband I've succeeded in snatching.) And search though she may, I won! This, of course, interrupted my eavesdropping, and then the call was over. But the candy was delicious.

Francine, though distracted by my journey to the bottom of the taxi, was intently listening to the phone conversation with the little French she knew and when the word "pistolet" was uttered Francine immediately tensed up and kicked Reynaldo so that she could mouth something to him.

"Forgive me, s'il vous plait, that was a friend of mine. I told him of my "bon chance" to have met the famous Winnie," said Marie-Christine.

"Excuse me, Miss. Miss! What route are you taking?" Reynaldo was studying the map on his phone and was expecting a much different route. "The Hotel de Vendôme is at Place Vendôme, why are we in Pigalle?" asked Reynaldo as he frantically looked out the window. They were very far off track.

"Ah! Le traffic, Monsieur. Le traffic! Excusez-moi, s'il vous plait, mais what does this light on my dashboard mean? Oh mon Dieu, the trunk is open! I must stop here for just a moment," said Marie Christine as she abruptly pulled over to the curb.

"Sure," said Reynaldo. "But, please, we're in a bit of hurry."

"Oui, Monsieur, this will only take a moment, and I assure you. You will arrive at the destination very soon," said Marie-Christine as she pulled the taxi to the curb.

At this point I was on the floor in my wheels in a secure position. Reynaldo and Francine were "on guard," Reynaldo definitely had anger in his voice when he asked, "Why are we in Pigalle?"

The taxi lurched to the right and stopped so suddenly that I almost tipped over. Reynaldo hit his head on the back of the front seat and Francine had to hold on to me with all her might.

Then Marie Christine jumped out of the taxi leaving the car door wide open. She ran to the back of the cab to close the trunk when two men jumped her, knocking her into the gutter. She screamed a muffled, quiet scream, almost as if she didn't want anyone to hear her. In rapid succession one of the men got behind the wheel while the other attacker pushed the groceries that were on the passenger seat to the floor, amazingly without spilling them, and pointed a gun at Reynaldo.

These men had angry voices and yelled at Francine and Reynaldo over and over. I was quite anxious about this. It was as if my primaries were being reprimanded for something, but I couldn't understand what it was. These men were speaking so frantically that all of their French, mixed with English, came out as a sonic blur. I could only register the hostile tone in their voices, not their words.

We rode along the street for another two minutes. Francine had picked me up off the floor and placed me on the seat between Reynaldo and herself. She was massaging my neck, trying to relax me but was unfortunately only transmitting fear. Fear and danger signals were all over the place and I experienced a feeling of which I've never liked to admit. I was scared and I wanted Francine and Reynaldo's protection.

I shuddered when the man in the front passenger seat hit Reynaldo with the gun. This was all so new to me. I had never witnessed human violence before; dog to dog, yes, but human to human? This was looming larger and larger in my head and my fear kept accelerating. I was in a panic and kept trying to get away from Francine's hold. I had to get out of that taxi. I needed to run fast and got my chance when the taxi finally stopped.

We pulled up to the sidewalk at the dead end of rue Chaptal. Both men got out of the taxi abruptly and slammed their doors. The sound was deafening. The man on Reynaldo's side grabbed him by the arm and yanked him out on to the sidewalk, and kept shoving him until they reached a plain, dark green, metal door off to the side of the main entrance of a large, semi-derelict brick building. It appeared that the building had once been a theatre, a centuries-old theater of the macabre.

Francine received the same treatment, but because she had lifted me onto her lap, wheelchair and all, I spilled on to the floor of the taxi when she was pulled from the car.

As she was being forced through the metal door, I gained the freedom I had sought earlier. But what kind of freedom was this. Too scared to wander, I pulled myself to the door ledge of the taxi on the curbside, over the hump in the middle, (we were sitting on the street side) and crawled out onto the sidewalk. No easy task, believe me. My wheels didn't want to roll over that doorsill and I had to pull with all of my strength. When my wheels were freed, they plopped down the eight inches to the sidewalk, killing my back.

Seemingly from out of nowhere, the man who had yanked Francine out of the taxi was standing over me. I tried to get away from him but he picked me up by my wheelchair's harness and threw me through the door Francine, Reynaldo, and the other man, had disappeared into.

What I'm about to say may mislead you into thinking I found this time in my life enjoyable. I didn't and it wasn't. But the truth is, I was about to embark on the greatest adventure of my life.

Behind the Green Door

The moment I stepped out of the bright Parisian daylight and into the total blackness inside the building, my eyes ached as they adjusted to their new circumstance. The green door slammed shut on its own accord, squeezing out the last sliver of light. I had to move very slowly because I couldn't see a thing, and could only guess where I might be, even though the four of them were moving quickly ahead into blackness relieved by the small beam of light from one of their flashlights.

After removing the disguise of large sunglasses and baseball caps, the men covertly doffed the hoods from their hoodies and donned black balaclavas. They then proceeded to force Francine and Reynaldo toward a passageway that descended by ramp down into yet another depth, and they kept pushing Reynaldo into railings and walls, yelling at both of them to move, move. When they reached a curved section, they all disappeared through a small doorway into an L shaped hallway and eventually into a large, dimly lit room with a table, metal shelving, a few cots with bedding, some chairs, and a case of bottled water on the floor. The room had one other door opposite the one we'd just entered through that was slightly ajar. I was the last to enter because the angle of the ramp made walking difficult and slow, although I must admit I was relieved not to be the leader.

The room was in the bowels of the old Le Théâtre du Grand-Guignol in what must have been the props and general storage rooms. Grand-Guignol was once famous for its gory horror plays. Gothic furniture of a somewhat battered condition with faded, torn fabrics of a bygone era along with realistic wax heads and body parts, all of which were shoved up against the walls to make room for the cots and provisions. The man who drove the taxi was organizing things with a sternness and command indicating anger that didn't seem to be pointed at us. Eventually he quieted down and turned his attention to the shelving, which held a tremendous amount of canned food, soft drinks, wine, and water. He was looking for something specific while complaining of not eating for the whole day.

Marie-Christine's henchmen, Laurent and Gilles, being good soldiers, were following her plan to the letter, except for two deviations; Gilles' wrestling her to the ground during the "car jacking", and Gilles (again) pistol whipping Reynaldo with such force that his health and wellbeing would become an unneeded burden. Consequently, Laurent's anger was pointed at Gilles.

"Put him on the cot by the door, and wipe the blood off his head!" Laurent commanded as he took some cans into the next room. Gilles did as he was told and Reynaldo winced at his touch. "And you didn't have to rough her up!"

"Well, she said make it look like a carjacking, so I did," said Gilles, trying to get Laurent to ease up on him. "In case someone saw us on the street. I thought it looked pretty real."

"I'll do that." said Francine. She was standing over the two of them holding back tears. "That was so stupid of you. You didn't have to hit him." She took the paper towel from Gilles and blotted away Reynaldo's blood. As she sat down on Reynaldo's cot, Gilles went over to the case of water and opened a bottle.

"Do you want to use this?" he asked, handing her the bottle.

"Thanks." She could see that Gilles had an ounce of remorse in him and that he might possibly be ashamed, or, more likely, worried about Laurent's opinion of him.

We took in our surroundings. The whole place was damp, dusty, and smelled moldy, and wrapped within this ambience was the odor of Reynaldo's blood. I perceived the fear and anger on Francine's part and then I perceived the strong odor of chicken cooking, possibly from behind the door Laurent had disappeared through.

This new chicken delight wafted to my nose and spoke to me. It said, "Come, Winnie, through this dark portal to extremely savory, flavorful chunks of chicken." The door in question, a rusty rectangle of metal, was only partially open, but wide enough for me, and my wheelchair, to squeeze through. Gilles, Francine, and Reynaldo, were completely occupied with keeping an eye on one another, so no one was watching me. There was no "Winnie, where are you going", or "Winnie, stay!" Nothing! And actually, from the outset the men never made any attempt to greet me, or even reach into one of their pockets for a treat. The only thing to ever come out of Gilles' pocket was the pistolet used to intimidate Francine and Reynaldo, although Reynaldo was beyond scared. Francine and Reynaldo were acting in ways much different from anything I had ever seen. He was lying on the cot, his speech slurred, and Francine was crying. But the chicken odor overrode everything else and I had to follow it to its source. In matters of food there simply is no choice.

And, really, I admit I wanted to get away from the violence, the yelling, the general mood, as much as I wanted that chicken. And I further admit that I'm prone to wander occasionally, and now I adamantly admit that I wish I would not wander, period.

Nothing good has ever come of it and I've always ended up the worse for it. But chicken! I had to find it.

As I exited the doom room, and got completely through the door, I saw Laurent in a poorly lit room with his back to me bending over a small, portable stove next to an old slate sink with mops and brooms leaning against it. He was cooking something from an opened can that had been discarded on the floor. He was intently focused on the steaming pots. In one of those pots was the chicken, or chicken like meat, with a seductive and distinctive aroma.

I wanted to ingratiate myself to him, to charm him into a handout, and so I did a sort of bark, but was ignored. I then thought he needed to see me. Enormous mistake! When I maneuvered around to get within his sight line, Laurent jumped and knocked over a chair, spilled one of the pots heating on the stove, the contents of which, a type of chicken stew that I wasn't familiar with, landed at my feet, I repeat at my feet! Extraordinary luck! I quickly got to work, and even though the chicken was very hot, it didn't burn my tongue, (a dog's tongue is a very different item from the one you're used to), and got quite a lot of it into my mouth before, OUCH! he kicked me in my right side. The chicken stew sprayed from my mouth as I ran, yes ran, wheels and all, out of there, through another rusty metal door, and into a vast and endless darkness farther away from Francine, Reynaldo, the two mean brothers, and the chicken.

Laurent called after me, shouting, "I haven't eaten since this morning, you mangy mutt." Then he called out in kind of an aside, saying, "Winnie, Winnie, come here, come here, girl!" He went into the room where everyone else was and complained about me. I stopped and considered heeding his call, sort of a pavlovian response I suppose, but a dog can tell when someone is insincere, so I kept on going.

Gilles Goes Shopping

"Your dog got away. She made me waste a whole can of cassoulet au confit de canard. Don't worry. I'll open another and she'll be back. She seems to love the stuff," Laurent said to Francine as he took down another can from one of the metal shelves lining the walls. He then turned his sights on Gilles who was sitting on the floor wiping a small amount of Reynaldo's blood from the side of his gun with a paper towel. He looked up and could see his brother's displeasure. The senseless violence that Gilles used on Reynaldo had changed the entire scenario the kidnappers had envisioned.

"We're going to need more paper towels. And get some toilet paper," said Laurent in a flat tone, just enough to show some disappointment in him. "Oh, and get another phone. And be sure to smash this one, don't just toss it after you've thrown out the sim card," said Laurent as he looked down on Reynaldo's feverish face. He wasn't doing well at all and the brothers didn't know what to do. They had him lying down and covered up. "And give me that gun."

It was left up to Gilles to watch Winnie. They each had a task, and Winnie was Gille's. He was always the dreamer, and he must have been dreaming of lunch when Winnie made her valiant run for what turned out to be the depths of the Parisian sewer system. Sending him on an errand would give Laurent a chance to figure out what to do with him. Francine had lunged for the door when Laurent said Winnie had run off, but Gilles caught her and threw her on to one of the cots, so he had his uses but Laurent would have to be ever more vigilant while by himself.

In the meantime they had to deal with Reynaldo. He must have suffered a concussion of some sort when Gilles hit him with the gun. He vomited and he couldn't stand up by himself. Francine was going crazy with worry, not only because of their immediate situation, but because of Reynaldo's condition and now, the loss of Winnie. The one thing Francine did have under control was what to do with a head injury, and she told them.

"Look, I've suffered a head injury so I'm pretty much an expert when it comes to this sort of thing. We need to let him lie here and rest. And tonight he's going to need to sleep as if these were normal times. Also, he can't be stressed any more than he already is, and please, just leave him alone so he doesn't have to make any decisions," Francine said as she sat down next to Reynaldo. "There's no medicine to take, not aspirin or anything else you might think he could take. He needs to get to a hospital. If there's internal bleeding then it has to be dealt with immediately. That's all we can do." Laurent and Gille stared at her as they realized how complicated things had become. "Why did your friend hit him?" she asked. "We were going where you wanted us to go. That was so unnecessary." Francine said as she looked from Laurent to Gilles who immediately looked at the floor.

"OK, that's enough," said Laurent. "*We'll* decide what to do with him. All you have to do is be quiet and not cause anymore trouble. This will all be over when our "request" is granted from your lawyer."

"Lawyer? What lawyer. You think we have someone on retainer?" Francine was getting mad now. "We're not some big corporation. We wrote a couple of books about a dog. That's it. You think there's a lot of money lying around somewhere? Listen, you two, we'd pay anything to get out of here, especially with Reynaldo passed out and Winnie running around out there scared out of her wits. There is no money for a ransom, unless you're not looking for much. We can give you a small amount, now!" she said, reaching into her purse. "Just ask. We want to get out of here! Really, you can have what we have, just let us go."

"Just calm down. I told you to be quiet, but since you have such a big mouth on you, just how much can you come up with? I mean now. What can you wire me?" asked Laurent. He was standing over Francine as close as he could without touching her.

"Around $60,000," said Francine.

"No. More like $50,000," Reynaldo mumbled from the cot. "This trip has already taken $10,000."

"Well, we'll take that. But I know you must have made some kind of money deal for the animation. And you get a steady stream of royalties for the two books. And I bet Winnie is insured. So don't tell me you only have $50,000. And if you want to see this thing end in a nice way, tell me who I can call to get a proper, let's call it a "settlement," Okay? Who should I call?" yelled Laurent. He had walked over to where Gilles was leaning on one of the metal shelves that held the ample supply of food and water. There were cans and cans of vegetables and fruits in syrup. Not to mention the confit and other assorted food. Nothing was fresh, nothing nice, nothing even hinting of the glorious French cuisine both Francine and Reynoldo were dreaming of enjoying with Paulette just a few hours earlier.

"There's no one."

"Give me your phone," Laurent demanded, as he emptied her purse out on the bed. He grabbed her iPhone and scrolled the contacts until he came to a french number.

"Ah! Voila! Who is this Paulette? Is she here in Paris? Tell me and I'll think about helping your husband. But she has to make this work, understand? Vraiment! We'll help him, if you get her to wire the money," snapped Laurent.

Gilles was leaving to do the shopping while this exchange was going on and thought to himself, 'Maybe I wasn't so off base after all. The husband is giving her the reason to move on this.' Which was now the only good part about hitting Reynaldo, but it also meant that he might be taken to a hospital. How, Gilles couldn't imagine. But there must be a way to do it. Laurent and Marie Christine would figure it out.

Out of the room, Gilles took off his balaclava, and entered the dark passages of the sewer. Once on the street he would feel more like himself. Stuck down below, being a kidnapper, being mean, wasn't easy. It wasn't him. He wanted it all over with as soon as possible.

Laurent went back to his stove to heat up another canned duck dinner and to contact Marie-Christine. He wanted to give her Paulette's phone number, and tell her about the $50,000 available right now if Paulette could wire it to the account Marie-Christine had set up. She also needed to know about Reynaldo's condition, and that they should think of a way to get him to a hospital.

A Pack of Truths

I'm the one. The leader. The one with all the answers. The one looked up to and depended upon. Why? I'll never know. I'm just me.

Born on to a cold concrete walkway in the sewers of Paris, sightless, like mom and my three siblings, I depended on her for everything, as a puppy should. She provided milk from her tummy and later rats and other "offerings" the sewers supplied.

When my two brothers and sister came along, I developed a little distance from my mom. I had a feeling that mom would not be here someday and then where would the food come from? So my instinct was to harden myself by not being available for her love-lickings or reprimands. Or perhaps it was just a case of my not liking being licked or reprimanded. In either case, I was different from the rest.

Eventually she left us by ceasing to exist. She decided to lie down and never get up again right in the middle of the cold concrete walkway upon which we were all born. And in her absence I became the new "mom" although by rights I should've been the new "dad" as I am a mister. By being different, aloof, independent, and a little grouchy toward anything near me, and maybe I should add smarter, too, I was the natural "next up" for the position of provider, protector, and ALPHA DOG.

Being a blind dog in a sewer system isn't a bad thing. I'm confident my nose more than makes up for a lack of sight. And my ears stick up very high in the air, so I'm able to hear better than most. A sewer life is a safe life, no cars or vehicles of any kind, no people (except one, I'll talk about him later), a constant temperature (58 degrees F), no rain, or snow, or a cold wind, or even sunshine for that matter, and my own tailor-made designations for day and night. Safe in all the natural earthly things but one. By that I mean the others. The others who are like us, even related to us, who would kill us and eat us if they could catch us. The cousins.

My siblings and I were all quite blind, all exceptionally large with a few more months of growing to go, and all very white. I always liked to imagine us as a large, white, blind pack of wolves. Wishful thinking, though, because we were actually of an ancient mix that had been fermenting down here for a century or more. And how did we manage that? The cousins of course. As you can see, it's complicated.

As brothers and sister, we all felt we looked very much alike, though we had never actually seen each other, (I should explain that we can "see" shapes and variations in light), but really, we are all pretty blind.

When it became my responsibility to feed my brothers and sister for that first hunger after mom ended, I instinctively trotted along the sidewalk next to the constantly running water to sniff out vermin. I learned this skill while tagging along with mom during her hunting routine. I was the only pup mom would allow to tag along during a hunt. I've always liked to think she sensed my destiny.

Right now I needed destiny to include a large rodent or two to satisfy all of the individual appetites, as the four of us were in a constant state of hunger. Growing as rapidly as we have since birth put a strain on mom, who needed to find enough rat and vole to fill four ever expanding adolescent bellies plus her adult one. This meant that she usually needed to find two or three vermin to fulfill her obligation to us. I had the same feeling of obligation to what has become my pack and I needed at least a very large male rat if I was to have any impact at all on my siblings growling stomachs.

So there I was, trotting very quietly, stealthily in fact, next to the highly malodorous stream of liquid that was the sewer, and was the water home to so many rats, mice, and voles. There was a rhythm here in the sound the rushing water made and what I listened for was any break in it. A slight change in sound was all I needed to pinpoint a living creature that might be swimming in the stream. I didn't have to identify what variety it was, I knew it was something to eat, but since it would have to feed four of us, I always listened for a size signature. I needed to hear some significant splashing, possibly a tail whipping the water as rats have a tendency to do to help with their equilibrium when the water was too fast. But so far the rhythm remained steady and monotonous.

I kept moving and took as long as I needed to find the right kill. I didn't have to guard the pack. My siblings and I were eighteen months old and skilled in the ways of canine defense. Our only enemy was that pack of cousins who were excessively fierce, but luckily, far away in the system. The four of them shared our traits but were older and bigger. We sensed that one, their leader, was jet black, based on the fact that we could only make out a dim silhouette of her body. The other three cousins were male.

Hunting was taking longer than usual and that tried the patience of my siblings, they were now right behind me. I could

do nothing about this, we were free to do as we pleased, and maybe they'd be of some help.

We enjoyed an abundance of vermin down here, so usually hunting was a pretty small part of the day. But for some reason no one was in the water. This meant something had scared them off. The water was the highway they used to get to their food. It also provided the nooks and crannies they called home. I could now hear that something was here and it was noisy. This thing didn't care about being stealthy, it literally clopped along the walkway, and had a rhythmic squeak, causing actual echoes up and down the tunnel. I heard it coming from up ahead, around a bend in the river. There was nowhere for me to hide so I hunkered down into an attack position. My siblings were in a perfect line close behind me. I was happy to see that we were all on the same page, all in a pretty good defensive lineup.

And then it appeared! I could make out the outline of either an exceptionally large rat with no tail and no back legs or, well, I just don't know what it was but the outline showed, now that it was closer, a small, low dog with wheels instead of back legs, ears like ours, a fine snout, and, hmm, I smelled a female, so, a female canine with wheels. We would normally tear this animal apart and eat it, but the wheels changed everything. They didn't smell like dog, I think there was human scent on them, and the whole package of this dog was just too strange. We had better be careful here. This animal didn't fit our expectations of normal prey.

So with caution, I slowly moved toward the animal, and did my sniff. OK. Pure dog. Seems weak, vulnerable, but the oddness of it has put attack off the table for the time being. My siblings moved in and the little beast actually snapped at my sister. It was a really good snap and we all jumped back. At this point the dog had her front legs out in front of her as if she wanted to play. All right. My brother took the bait and did some play dancing, but this animal didn't respond in kind. She just lay there. It seemed

that the dog didn't want to play, she wanted to sleep. And on closer inspection, I smelled blood. She had a raw wound on her haunch. Well, she can sleep all she wants, though I think that if she did she wouldn't last the night. We couldn't worry about this stranger, we needed food so we moved on. And she followed.

Please be aware of how extraordinary this night was turning out to be. Meeting a dog down here was a very special event. This dog posed no threat, so we were mildly happy to have her with us. I could tell she was older, calmer than the rest of us. She had an air of "world weariness" akin to my mom's persona. And, even though she snapped at my sister, she wanted our company too. So our hunt turned out to be more interesting than usual, but frustratingly, not bountiful at all. I could only partially blame wheel dog for the lack of vermin. It didn't make sense that her meandering in the brick tunnels of the sewer would have caused such a large-scale exodus of rats and voles. There had to be some other strange thing going on down here.

My siblings and I have intense olfactory abilities and we were on high alert to find that group of out of place molecules that would give us a hint as to what was going on. We had moved into another tunnel system, seemingly narrower because of the sound reflecting off the walls. The water here was moving slower and was less odiferous. I picked up a slight variation of the odors in the air. I smelled vermin. Finally, something. But wait a second. What's this? Not vermin, I think I smelled a human! This group of lingering odor molecules were definitely from a man.

We were stalking now. All of us lifted our feet off the ground in slow motion and stayed very low to the ground, like synchronized swimmers. The human smell was intense. I could make out a silhouette of someone lying down. Face down. Our human was a man lying face down on the cold cement walkway next to the sewer. He was moaning, rubbing his head where a deep, red gash had interrupted a perfect covering of blond, shiny hair, and he was shaking all over. And everywhere was the scent of blood.

Wheeldog went right up to him and licked his head. Crazy! But the man did nothing and wheel dog continued licking. Then he stirred. He rolled over to one side to see Wheeldog who then licked his neck. The man reached out to her and gently petted her head. He got up on one elbow and saw the rest of us. We froze. You never knew with humans. But he spoke to us in soothing tones.

Encouraged by his benevolent sounds and his seductive petting of Wheeldog, we, one by one, went over to him and sniffed. Soon the man sat up and we, in total character reversal, being such big, strong, independent dogs, gathered around him hoping that he would pet us too. None of us, I repeat, none of us have ever been petted, nor have we ever encountered close human contact. This happened as a result of some deep instinct and we were no longer in control. We are what we are, albino mutt puppies, and we still needed to fill the void of affection left by the absence of our mother. We needed whatever love this human could give us.

The Sky Is Falling

ALAIN PICARD

I've always believed everyone's had a main event. Something, no matter how good or bad, that happened, either through one's own design or by happenstance. And when you've looked back over your life, it's usually not too hard to pinpoint it. For example, maybe you were in a war and you saved or killed someone, or perhaps it was something as wonderful as meeting your future wife. Whatever form it took, it stood out in your mind. You never forgot it.

I thought my main event was going to be a positive and wonderful thing. The stars were aligned to favor Alain Picard, or AP, as I was usually referred to. I was vibrating with excitement and anticipation. Though a little bit boring to those around me, all I could think of or talk about was what I thought was going to be my main event.

My profession was dancer for the Paris Opera Ballet. The result of a journey of many kilometers from Roussillon, a small hill town in Provence, and 18 years of study and hard work at the Paris Opera Ballet School. From quadrille to coryphée to sujet, my progress was steady and, I thought, predictable. Then I attained premier danseur status and my art flourished. Some hidden barrier broke within my psyche and I couldn't be stopped. I was destined to be a star.

On the day of my performance of the role of James in La Syphide it became official; I was told by Sylvie Aubert, the director of the Paris Opera Ballet that she would announce my new status within the company before that night's performance. I was to be named an "etoile." This designation put me at the highest echelon of dancers. And though I was overwhelmed, I secretly expected nothing less and couldn't wait to get on stage to dance as a "star." Alain Picard – ETOILE. Could this be my "main event?"

Eighteen years of one thing, one very major thing, has had its drawbacks. At age twenty-six I knew nothing other than dance; the leçons, the venues, rehearsals, cigarettes, aches and pains, pills, chit-chat, politics, and sweat. And other than gossip consisting mostly of "shop talk," I had no real relationship with other people. My parents were gone and I had no other family. This singularity seeped into my psyche and left it with a preference for avoiding anything that could be construed as a friendship. I couldn't seem to let anyone get past my profession, not even myself. AP was definitely a loner.

As a result I was torn. On one hand dancing was completely fulfilling. It was a perfect way to spend one's life. On the other, it did make you feel a little strange compared to the average guy. And if you took a look at me, you'd see that I had everything. I was fairly decent looking, I'd attained etoile status for the Paris Opera Ballet, and I was able to interact pleasantly enough with those I worked with. I even had a sense of humor, and it wasn't the least bit cynical! But I knew myself well, and deep within there was nothing of interest that I had to offer. I was embarrassed to be me.

It was true that when it came to meeting a fan, a trustee, or any one of the many authority figures lurking about the Palais Garnier, I would utilize my easy-going attitude and act as agreeably and confidently as anyone could. In general I had them all fooled. Fooled because I had an underlying distrust of all of this good fortune, a sense that it could end at any moment, as it had for several of my dance mates.

Of course, without any reservation, my favorite place to be was on the stage. But my second favorite was the food table, and at the Palais it was located down two ramps in a spooky cellar that always felt damp and dark. The food table was so located because the vast refrigeration rooms for the kitchens of the Palais's restaurant, L'Opera Restaurant, were there and so it was easy for the kitchen staff to deposit random "snacks" for any of us to take at will. Along with the mandatory full lunch as stipulated by our contract, the kitchen staff also offered beautiful creations, leftovers and experiments, almost always incredible and definitely most welcome. All of us looked forward to our quick trips to "the table." Dancers are a voracious lot and those trips were one of the little things you kept in the back of your mind to keep you going while killing yourself during rehearsal.

The food table was a tradition that began in the late 1600s to feed the dancers and the theater hands what was most likely their only meal of the day. The offerings were hardy, nourishing bowls of basic food necessary to keep them from fainting during performances for the various royals in attendance.

Presently, when I'd scurry down to "the table" during rehearsal, I'd generally find no one there as we all had different things to work on at different times. So my moments of solitude and fine dining took place in this dingy, ancient place with eerie sounds, endless tunnels, and rusty doors leading to other, scarier places I chose to ignore.

On the day of the big performance, I wasn't eating. My

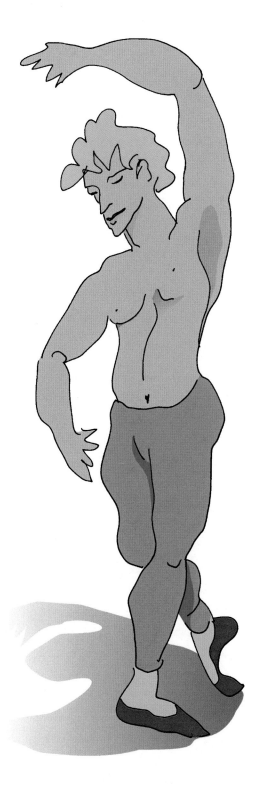

stomach wouldn't have been able to deal with food and butterflies at the same time. Sure, I might faint as a result of malnourishment, but I was so intent on this performance that I knew I would spring to life when my time came.

Finally, we had come to my main event and were about to begin our performance of La Sylphide. I was in position, stage left, near the very back, sitting at a desk and after my fiancé, Effie, and the Sylph both finished their kisses, I was to execute a *grand jete* preceded by a *coupe* during the opening movement, to a point center stage, with a single spotlight on me. Beyond that I had no idea. My mind was a blank. I've blanked out before and I refused to worry, my role would reveal itself as needed and then it would be done. It was in the mind of my muscles.

The conductor, Frederico Sunjin, tapped his baton on the podium; we were about to begin. My concentration was so intense that I noticed nothing around me except Giselle and Anna on either side of me. They would follow me downstage with pliés until I reached position. This task didn't allow for any intrusions on my concentration whatsoever, and that included the lighting technician forty feet above me, adjusting a spotlight that had come loose from its stay-clamp and bathed the front of the stage with a sweep of unintended, brilliantly white light.

Maestro Sanjin's musical cue had propelled me forward. My timing was incredible (if I say so myself). I knew I was giving a near great performance, based on two things: One; I was gliding and floating across the stage, two; absolutely nothing hurt. What I was doing, what I was experiencing was so astoundingly wonderful. It was an indescribable feeling of being complete. All I could think about was how much I loved to dance, loved my body, and loved the fact that for these few minutes (maybe for the whole performance) I wasn't worried about what others may have thought about me. But wait? What was that? There came a jarring sound, and not from the orchestra. And the lighting cues were

different from those in rehearsal. The beam of intense white light from my spotlight was moving wildly about the stage, getting brighter, getting closer.

That was where my memory of that night ended. From a

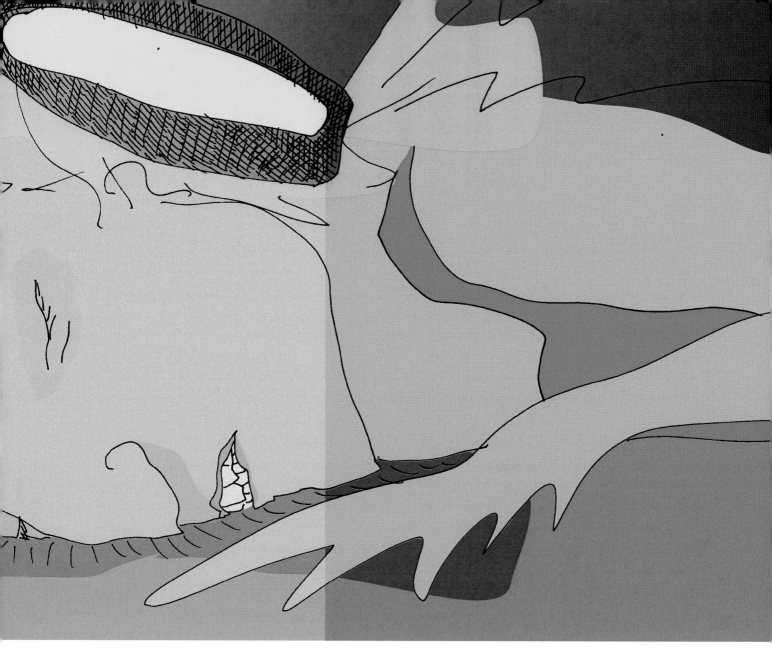

bright, white light to complete black in an instant. I only knew what happened because I awakened seconds later to the voices around me recounting "the event." A spotlight fell and hit ME! It hit ME! ME, just when I was feeling the world was mine. ME, when my mind and body were so much in tune that I wasn't even self-conscious. ME, when I had danced perfectly to the front and center of the stage, the center of everything. I was finally, for the first time in my life, the center of everything!

And then, bang and slice, my real "main event" began. My fairly decent looking face was suddenly all over the place. I felt sick with pain. Totally confused and disorientated, my instinct told me to get up and get away from this pain, away from the audience, away from whatever caused this awful feeling. My embarrassment overtook my physical pain. There I was, the center of attention, not because I was a living work of art, or even an element of a work of art, but because I was a freakish spectacle.

While profusely bleeding all over my blouse, jacket and plaid kilt, I actually jumped up. I remembered this all to well. I jumped up and ran to stage right, out into the wings and then to the ramps leading to the table. Not to eat, believe me, I was too sick to my stomach to think of food, but to find a place to lick my wounds in solitude. Everyone around me was in as much shock as I was. No one followed me and I disappeared through one of the many rusty old doors leading to what I discovered was a maze of tunnels.

My face was struck by that spotlight. My right eye was bleeding, and half of my face felt as though it had been scraped away. My cheek-bone felt as though it was broken. I couldn't even imagine touching my head because I was in too much. . .blah, blah, blah, no need to go on and on, you can imagine what I was going through.

My left eye was working. It had come to this. I was dependent on my left eye. My arms and my left leg worked, my right leg seemed to have slowed the lamp's journey by allowing a sharp piece of it to slice me on its way to the stage floor. I wanted to die. The pain was unbearable, and I thought what will I be when or if the pain goes away? A freak! I couldn't think about that now. I was losing a lot of blood. I was so scared and in a total state of confusion and panic. I had to stop the bleeding and my confused brain was not helping. It was saying "get out of here! Go through this door into yet another tunnel. Don't let anyone see you. Go, now, I can hear them coming!"

But that was panic speaking, taking control, making decisions. What I should have done was crawl back up to the stage and gotten help. But panic ruled and so I shoved yet another ancient, rusty door open. I stumbled through, because that's how graceful I'd become, stumble, lunge, trip forward, into a long, endless tunnel where I moved slowly forward, away from the door, away from those who might have followed me down here, away from my old life and toward a new life, filled with promise and hope. A life….what am I saying? This was the gateway to hell. This was the sewer of Paris.

I was still functioning, but it was only my panic functioning. I was in shock. I wasn't my usual self, that's for sure. And then I started to shake like crazy. The pain was causing me to move, as if I was going to escape it if I kept moving forward. I was compelled to keep going deeper into the darkness.

I must have been quite a sight, blood everywhere, face severely scraped, crimson legged, and limping. I thought, I really shouldn't be down here, I should be trying to get back to people and get help. That would've been the logical thing to do. But I was a little cocky about the "etoile" business, and being self-conscious, I couldn't get up the nerve to face anyone in my repulsive, needy condition. And besides, I seemed to have been drawn to the coolness down here. I thought it might feel good to lie down on the cement walkway and rest for a few moments. I only needed to travel a little farther down, maybe to that opening a few feet ahead.

I thought back to my performance and my life up to a few moments ago and I cried. The tears were so painful, you have no idea. The stinging pain, brought about by my obliterated tear duct trying to do its job, was causing me to lunge blindly forward through an opening in the tunnel. I was thinking that finally I was now very well hidden in the sewer system. Tucked securely away in the bowels for the bowels. My supply of adrenaline had finally given out. I was no longer able to muster any energy. My brain was shutting down and was seeking a place to go blank, to give up. There was just enough something to push me a little farther and then to lie down and rest. That's what was needed now. Lie down and rest. My demented rationale was saying very convincingly that really AP, these wounds were not that bad, just small stuff. I just needed to rest now. Right here. This would do. I needed to lie on my face…needed the cool cement on it. Need to close my eyes. Needed to……

A Bridge to Nowhere

Francine was carrying me in her usual over the shoulder configuration with my head looking back as she moved forward down the corridor. I was a little tired and being carried, though it did feel good to be so close to Francine, my ear next to her ear, was an effort because I had to use muscles rarely disturbed in my everyday routine. Being held close to her body placed me in an up and down position as if I were sitting up. With her support I could manage, but only for a short while before it became quite painful. My two front legs and paws were clamped over her shoulder and were ready to give, when finally, we reached our compartment.

She carefully, and it was always carefully, Francine was incredibly sensitive to my situation, laid me down on the soft, reddish-brown plush velvet seat that was as long as a sofa, spanning the width of the highly polished dark wood compartment. I was on my back and the tips of my ears touched the soft padded seat back.

Francine had settled in next to Reynaldo and they were both removing their footwear. Seated across from me, I was feeling a little disappointed not to be between them when, plop! two pairs

across the Atlantic Ocean to the center of London was conjuring up many memories that I didn't know I had.

As I laid in this womb-like, wonderfully comfortable, wonderfully secure position, with the sounds produced by the train's wheels speeding on the tracks below on this long, high bridge over the ocean, my eyes opened, then closed over and over, each time a little more closed than open, and my mind drifted in a dream that carried me to the spot in the Atlantic that we were presently traveling over. This was the place where the plane crashed. A crash that I miraculously survived. This was the very spot in the Atlantic where I lost sight of Francine and Reynaldo. This was where Francine received the deep gash on her forehead. And this is where I began my long swim to Brighton Beach, England.

As these memories wafted up like little bubbles in a bathtub, I pierced them by biting at them, in my mind of course, to get at the thoughts inside. This one was of me swimming. The cold and the wet, the birds tearing me apart, the dark, the hunger, the taste of the blood and the salt water, all things of the past and usually well buried in my simple psyche, but on this train, on this plush seat with Francine and Reynaldo so strong a presence across from me, I seemed to be so relaxed that I could see the past, a past that included Francine's distinctive forehead indentation, the result of a piece of luggage striking her during the violent upheaval caused by the plane crash. I didn't see that happen. I couldn't find her that night. I only know about it from hearing her speak of it to Reynaldo and somehow it registered, hidden deeply within 'til this night.

Oh! Now this little bubble contained the Queen. This is definitely a warm happy bubble because the Queen was so nice to me. And look, there's Vulcan. I like remembering Vulcan, the Queen's dorgi, and our fight. It was so much fun. I could actually feel his bite on my haunch, exactly as if it were really happening right now. I could feel this bite quite intensely. This bite was taking

of ankles and feet snuggled in on either side and held me in. Their feet, in thick wooly socks, Francine's with Corgis all over them, Reynaldo's completely nondescript, warm and soft, were adorned with a tasty odor.

As we began our journey, the train gently rocked forward, lurched, then rolled backward for it's first tentative movement, but then reversed and settled on forward for its long, non-stop rolling course to our destination, England.

That special trip, that special train, departing from the station in Wilmington Delaware, and traveling over the high bridge me away from my train trip to England. This bite really hurt!

That really hurt! I barked this. I've no lips capable of forming those words. Nor a larynx and vocal chords capable of the resonance needed to make my bark sound like the words "that really hurt," so I was left to bark this phrase, and loudly. And then my eyes opened. I was wide-awake and ready for action. Apparently I had been sleeping deeply and dreaming. But soon I was totally alert and fully pumped with adrenaline.

Blinking a little, I looked around for the source of my pain. I was in my wheels with my head in a chin down position, my body on the cold cement with my front legs splayed out as wide as possible, and my posterior was up, suspended by my wheels. I was trying to see what was biting me when two large rats scurried out from behind and jumped into the water. I checked my painful right haunch and saw blood.

Normally this would not have been a big deal as I would simply lie down, curl around and settle in to a nice "lick my wounds to coagulation" session. A simple "lick-me-by" as Reynaldo would call it. We dogs love this and usually forget about the event that brought us these joyful moments. With the wheel chair, though, that would be very difficult because I can't curl around and make these bites heal or stop bleeding.

Standing up on the walkway I'd been traveling on for seemingly quite some time, and sensed that I had company other than the rats. My nostrils were on full alert, and the odor was comforting and familiar, though a little stronger than I was used to. It was the unmistakable odor of a dog or, more accurately, dogs.

The walkway was full of twists and turns. Some portions were lighted and some were so dark I might as well have been blind. Sometimes it was dry and smooth, but usually it was slimy and peppered with piles of sewage, raw and otherwise. And always to my left was the smelly river, the sewer.

The sewer's odors were all the "off" odors that I would have naturally found intriguing. For the most part the pungency approached overwhelming, and I liked this. The other rivers I had experienced were without any discernible odor. This one was truly ripe and so strong that I was amazed that I was able to smell the canines now coming toward me.

They were four, they were big, and they were strange. These dogs were a pack. No mistaking that. They walked in single file. You could readily see the pecking order. Granted, there was nothing unusual about dogs in pack form, and actually that's the ideal dog's life, to be part of a pack. What was strange though, was the color of their eyes. Their eyes were practically white. Did they see me? I know they must have smelled me, they're dogs after all. But did they *see* me?

Well, it turned out that they could sort of see me, smell me, and pretty much everything else me. These dogs were intensified in all things canine. One male, the first in the pack, the leader, approached with a minimum of caution, probably because I didn't fit the normal canine profile — you know, head, body, four legs to the ground, and a nice tail sticking up. My wheelchair had him flummoxed. And I say probably because the way it works in the dog world, I, an intruder into what I'm pretty sure was this guy's territory, would be attacked. I think my wheels were saving me.

He sniffed me the way we dogs do, and I just stood there helpless and not feeling any of my old alpha self. I was too tired. He sniffed some more and then the others came over and nosed me to the point where I was getting annoyed. OK. Enough. I did a small snap, just enough to show that I wasn't a complete pushover. They jumped back a little, then one of them made like he wanted to play. Play? I can't play. I can barely stand. We were just sort of at stand off in terms of what to do. The lead male was losing interest in me and the others were prone to follow his lead, and I was ready to be a follower at this point, so we just headed off, to who-knew-where.

I See the Light Come Shining

The man and my four pack mates offered little comfort while I was in their company. Everyone was in survival mode. Everyone was either in pain or hungry, or both in my case, and though I could sense a casual looking out for each other in the pack, the group of six as a whole fell under the heading "every man for himself," even us girls!

As I dragged myself along the dark walkway, I heard extraneous splashing in the rushing, dank void posing as a river and tried imagining what could possibly be enjoying a swim in such a foul soup. But whatever it was, and my mind jumped to the biting rats that had decimated my right haunch, it stimulated the lusty carnivore in me that I had kept hidden all of these years. So, whoever was doing laps next to me was now officially a candidate for my imaginary food bowl.

In the distance, and I do mean far, far away, I could only just make out a confetti square of light. It wasn't the same hue of yellow light that had been illuminating my journey, either, which indicated to me that it wasn't more of the bare light bulbs strung up on the ceiling of this concrete and brick cavern every twenty Corgi lengths or so. This light was blood red! I haven't recalled ever seeing light like this, but that was not even a consideration in my dog's brain. Truly, light was light and I had never taken notice of the color. As a matter of fact, I didn't really see the light as blood red, it looked egg yellow to me, blood red was how *Dogspeak* chose to describe it because it registered at 700 on the nanometer scale, which to a human, and a computer program,

is red. But now, in my worn-out state, my thoughts were looking for any signpost signifying a difference, a change from the endless, hungry, and painful wandering I'd been enduring for too many lost meal-times. So in my mind a new light source with a new light color meant a new experience ahead. And hope! I finally had some hope. And this hope was making me drool in anticipation of the possibility of food.

Well I shouldn't say food was a possibility. I was just crazed at this point, and absolutely anything would have made me drool. I may have been drooling about the animals in the water beside me. I may have contracted rabies! No, just kidding, I didn't feel rabid. But I wasn't myself. That was a fact. Putting my mental state aside for the moment, my physical side was even worse: haunch — killing me; stomach — wouldn't shut up; front paws — aching and bleeding from the rough concrete walkway. And my mental state? Well, we've already covered that. So it was understandable how this confetti of red light at the end of the blackness in which I was immersed could conceivably produce a drool. And I shouldn't even have to justify drooling for heaven's sake. As anyone could see, I was getting grouchy.

For me that goalpost of light, literally the light at the end of the tunnel, was something to be accomplished with unimaginable gains in store for the lucky one who passed through it, and that was all I could think of. But the other five, my tunnel mates, human and dogan, had other goals, other ideas, and other fantasies and strategies as to how to make this tunnel thing work.

They veered off to the left, into an opening I didn't even see, and left me to my destiny.

How did I feel at this moment, being left on my own, alone in a dark tunnel with an ever-enlarging rectangle of light as my only point of focus? Optimistic, that's how I felt. Finally there was something to accomplish — get to the light and quite possibly be free of this nightmare. That was all I had, and for me that was enough. You see, Instinctualism was my religion. Instinct was my god, and He was telling me to move forward as quickly as my tattered body could go. And as I did I noticed the light getting bigger and bigger, brighter and brighter, and so red (intensely yellow to me) that I had to admit to a little fear. But fear was not going to stop a direct order from the all mighty Instinct, and as I approached it I could see a wall that was not smooth concrete or neatly finished bricks. I'd forgotten that other types of walls existed, and this one was made of huge, bumpy rocks, each one easily twice the size of a Corgi. My red (yellow) light was coming from a human-sized opening cut into the stone fitted with a metal door, only slightly ajar and not wide enough for my wheels to squeeze through. Of course, that was why we have snouts, and with mine I nudged the door a tad to open it a wider, with much pain I might add, but because it was a metal door and rusty at that, it had little inclination to move from its resting place. So it was with great relief that I discovered I wasn't so completely alone after all.

With snout firmly positioned against the cold metal of the door and with flaps, teeth, and gums aching from the amount of pressure I was exerting, I heard above the roar of the sewer river rushing by, the sound of a shuffling man not in control of his cadence. I quickly turned my head to see him with the pack of four, who had somehow emerged from a doorway a few Corgi lengths behind me.

The man's eyes reflected the reddish light seeping out from the open space the door had provided. His face, full of non-human crags and crevices, was a maze of reddish to black shadows that created a curious affect. Most importantly, his face smelled of blood and as you may remember, I had licked same from him earlier and had really liked it.

The next most important fact was that since we had already met, I had no fear of this person. I was sensing a sort of camaraderie in our mutual circumstance. But beyond these fleeting thoughts, fleeting because I was determined to get through this door and possibly closer to food and freedom, I was receiving some really impressive alpha signals from this fellow. Feelings I hadn't felt since being with Francine, and to a lesser degree, Reynaldo, and to an even lesser degree from the pack's leader. I was actually relaxing a little and sensed this person was going to take care of me in some unimaginable way.

He knelt down next to me with great effort because he seemed to have pain in his legs similar to my pain, and petted me. Petted me? I didn't need petting at this stage, I needed a meal. But maybe he needed to pet something warm and furry — in other words me! Who knew in these times of deprivation. I felt his loneliness and gentleness, but also some kind of burbling rage, not directed at me, but most likely the rage of pain that tainted the gentle stroking he bestowed upon me.

And then, with an abrupt rush of adrenaline, the petting was terminated and with a quick movement while still kneeling beside me, he opened the door to its fullest extent and of which I took the fullest advantage.

Keep Your Eyes on the Road

She swore at Gilles for knocking her to the gutter. He looked horrified and frightened. He hadn't meant to go that far. She could tell he was not cut out for this, so nervous, jittery, and out of control. Marie-Christine just lay there, in the gutter on Rue Chaptal until they moved on to the end of the street. She watched as they skidded to a halt and got out of the cab. She saw Gilles pistol-whip Reynaldo, and watched him falter and stagger. It was too much, too hard of a hit. Where the hell did that come from? There wasn't supposed to be any violence. This looked bad.

She got up, brushed herself off, straightened her wig and re-tied her scarf. Then she walked quickly to her taxi. Laurent must have been nervous, too, because he left the engine running. Lucky Rue Chaptal was a quiet street.

She made a U-turn at the end, passing the old theater, and the green door next to it. It seemed like a good time to break her one cigarette a day rule and with hands shaking, lit up. She proceeded into the midday traffic on her way back to her apartment. The phone rang and she picked it up. Her left hand had the wheel and the cigarette, her right thumb answered the phone, and both sides of her brain had a headache.

It was Laurent, of course. He was whispering and she could barely make out what he was saying. He sounded pissed off. He was mad at Gilles, and felt like he had to do everything himself. "Gilles let Winnie escape into the sewer. We'll never see her again," he said. "Take this number." And he told her Paulette's phone number. "They'll wire $50,000 into that account you set up."

"OK. Wait. OK, I have the number in my phone, but, listen, there's more than $50,000. Lots more. I don't want to keep calling to make these transactions. It'll be best to do just one contact for the whole thing, whatever it is," said Marie-Christine adamantly.

"No, aunt. Listen to me. This may be all we can get. This Paulette is going to call someone in the states who's going to have to arrange getting the money somehow. And all that without getting the police involved. I say we should just do the 50 Gs and get it over with." Laurent was at the stove heating food for the four of them.

Marie-Christine took this in. She knew he was making sense, but she also knew they had taken a huge risk and $50,000 didn't seem to be the right amount of payback. She was about to present her thoughts to Laurent when a motorcycle cut in front of her causing her to swerve the Mercedes into a truck travelling way too fast through city. It broadsided her taxi and flipped it over. Marie-Christine had forgotten to fasten her seat belt in her excitement and was thrown against her side window with such force that her head smashed into it. She ended up alive on the sidewalk, but unconscious.

Laurent heard the whole thing and was yelling "Auntie, Auntie", but of course, all conversation was over between those two. Now he really didn't know what to do. He was frantic. She was so important to him and Gilles. Actually, she was all they had. They were very close. He assumed it was some sort of crash, but how would he find out?

On top of that, he was afraid to leave Francine and Reynaldo with Gilles, because, who knows, he might let them go, or kill them, or just run away. And calling Paulette himself was something he hadn't planned to do. Lauarent thought, "We each have a job in this, our own part to play. Gilles will watch over Winnie and be the outside person for the pickup, I will take care of all inside activities, including cooking, bathroom breaks, etc and getting vital information from them, and auntie will be the voice of the operation." Marie-Christine was to make the money call.

When Gilles got back, Laurent filled him in. Gilles wanted to go out to see what he could find out. He thought maybe he should go to her apartment. She might be there. Her phone may be damaged and that's why she wasn't picking up. And if she isn't there, maybe a neighbor had heard something. At any rate, he'd feed Evelyn and Schnitzel if she hadn't come home. There was certainly no information coming to this dungeon. And so he left.

After Gilles left, Francine got up from Reynaldo's cot and went out to talk to Laurent. She'd heard everything. "What happened?" she asked.

Laurent was a white as a blizzard. He didn't use his tough guy talk but just said, "Someone's been in a car accident." He was still holding the phone and stirring a pot of one the canned meals that lined the shelves in the other room. He put the phone down next to the stove and faced Francine.

"You need to go back to the other room. I don't want you to talk to either of us," he said quietly. "Later tonight you're going to call your friend Paulette and make arrangements to wire that money to us." He looked down at the phone. He stared at it for a long time. And then he realized how stupid this whole thing had been. He didn't know the bank account number, only Marie-Christine did. Nor did he know the transfer codes. The whole thing was a fiasco. He was defeated and in so much trouble. The American would get them for sure if the police didn't.

He called Gilles to find out anything he might know, but there was nothing to tell. She wasn't there and no one had heard anything about a car crash. They both tried to think of her possible route to her apartment and what hospital would be likely to take an emergency patient on that route.

Someone Left the Cake out in the Rain

I was making coffee. I had a morning routine, probably identical to yours. I'd wake up but lie in bed for approximately 20 minutes and think about getting up. Then I'd actually sit up, swing my legs out of bed, put on my robe, make the necessary bathroom stop, and then go into the kitchen. In my cupboard I kept two things: sugar and coffee. Other than that the cupboard was bare. I'd grab the kettle and fill it while looking out the window into the windows of other people's apartments across the courtyard, seeing them in various stages of much the same activity, making me feel as though I was a part of a group, or maybe even part of a family. This was a tremendous comfort to me.

Then I'd drink the coffee, but not in my apartment. No, I was magically transported to "the table," my home away from home with the coffee in a paper cup sporting star drawings all over it. And there was cake, sliced perfectly into slim, triangular slices resembling tongues so that the human hand could grasp a slice, hold it without it breaking, and place it into one's mouth in one go. Propped up behind the table was a gigantic Louis XIV mirror with an elaborate gilt frame. The mirror had been there forever and as I reveled in the comfort of my coffee and cake I glanced at my image. I saw a tall young man possessing some discrete muscular definition about the arms and torso. His legs were not visible because of the table, but the face would be if it weren't for the lamp illuminating the table, that hung right at neck level, leaving my face a mystery.

My cake wasn't behaving properly the way it should've. It was cut in a sliver shaped portion and I should've been able to eat it in two bites. But my cake was licking me, and was very moist. Each lick caused some really intense pain. And with this pain came the realization that I wasn't standing up eating cake and drinking coffee. I was on my stomach, with my face pressed against the cold cement walkway in a Paris sewer, coming out of a mini-coma and being licked by a Corgi.

I was being licked by a handicapped Corgi, a female, if I wasn't mistaken, licking me right on my worst spotlight wound, and it was killing me. I pushed her away and she mercifully stopped. I couldn't figure this out. How could a dog be down here licking me, a dog in a wheelchair yet! I could barely think straight to begin with and now this was thrown at me. Behind her I saw four more dogs, bizarre white ones with eerie, white eyes. I was still so self-absorbed with my pain and circumstance that I could only just take this in. I wasn't even concerned about this seemingly wild pack of four dogs, intently studying me. Maybe I was too used to an audience.

An ingrained survival instinct told me to sit up and at least appear larger than they were, although those white dogs were huge. I was hesitant because I thought I might vomit, and couldn't allow myself to appear vulnerable in front of my new friends. I propped myself up with my arms, which were working normally. I sat up and immediately got dizzy, so I put my head down low to alleviate some of the whirling and spinning my

brain was doing when the Corgi came close to my head. She wanted to lick my wounded face afresh. I wanted nothing to touch my face and besides, what was her motive? Could it have been that this is the way animals heal their wounds and she just wanted to help me? I knew there was something about their saliva but I couldn't think of it now so I again pushed her away.

Eventually one of the other dogs came over. This dog was a monster, made all the more so by being so white. Some quick thinking was required, something I wasn't ready to do. But I needed to establish some sort of boundary or respect from these animals. All I could come up with was a mumble of "good boy." It came out "oo oy." I couldn't work my jaw or my lips. It hurt but I kept going "oo oy, oo oy." And Oo oy responded. He came over and did some sniffing, then licked me. On my face! I've won him over and it was killing me. I decided that, as sick as I felt, I was going to have to get physical with these guys. I petted his snout while gently pushing him away from my face. He melted and climbed right onto my lap, and I think I mentioned, he was big. My bleeding leg, which I think had coagulated along what I had named the Mariana Trench, had now reopened for business with old Oo oy wiggling around as I petted him.

I'd never had a dog so this was all new to me. As a matter of fact everything that night was new to me. One by one, the three other big, white dogs lifted their large paws and cautiously approached my worn out, wasted body. And one by one they gave me a sniff and then a good licking, in the most loving way.

Amazingly, they were so gentle. This perplexing situation was invading my psyche, for I had never actually experienced such warm feelings of love before. In terms of my physical pain, I was in agony, but emotionally, I was being lifted to a new and wonderful plane while leaving behind my self-pity. I was actually enjoying myself.

Soon I was swimming in a pool of four large, white dogs all vying for my affection. If only I didn't feel so awful, what a party this would have been. They, of course, had no idea how much this hurt, with all of their jostling and licking, and they were becoming exceedingly happy and playful. The Corgi was keeping her distance, thank god, and was moving down the tunnel to a point where she just disappeared from sight. The White Dogs and I were now sort of on the same intellectual level because I could barely think a complete thought and they were just gaga over me.

But somewhere in my brain, in a part that wasn't busily screaming the message of OUCH, one small synapse vesicle was dumping neurons of thought, important survival thought, to a receptor that had been waiting for something more stimulating than ouch. The dumped neurons were heavy with the thought of telling my legs to get me to at least "the table" and even farther along if possible. I knew this didn't sound like much, and the dog play must have made everything look so normal and happy, but the truth was we were a new, but completely dysfunctional family and this obvious move to get out of the sewer was nothing but a stroke of genius, relatively speaking. We chose to follow that Corgi.

Food for Thought

I was the first one through the door. The others, the man, the white quartet, all followed me into the unknown. The man stopped abruptly and said as best he could "I smell something. I think it's the food table. We're going the right way, you little corgi. We're on our way to the Ballet!" He was very excited, considering his condition. The words came out a little misshapen, a little garbled, but they were loud and with emphasis, which was a positive sign.

The man and I dragged ourselves toward the food smell while the others trotted ahead. In a few minutes we could hear some commotion in the distance, which could only mean that they had reached the food. There was much barking and growling and I could hear plates and bowls crashing to the floor.

When we arrived, most of the food at the food table was on the floor and the four whites were all over it. But it was a plentiful spread and I dove in with tremendous gusto. The man didn't partake in our party, either because he couldn't tell which food had bits of broken crockery in it, or he was simply not hungry. But for whatever reason, he ignored the feast and limped toward a ramp leading up to a higher level. When he reached the base of the ramp he stopped and turned to look at us. A feeling of supreme loss went through him as he realized he most likely would never see "the pack" again. Never feel love like that again. The reality of what his future held started to seep into his psyche and it was with utter sadness that he crawled up the ramp to the wings of his future.

I, having feasted, having chomped on everything the albino demolitionists threw to the floor, was, along my with dinner mates, feeling nauseous from eating too fast, and bloated from eating to much. So for me, one more favor was requested, the freedom from my rolling prison. My urge to be free of my wheelchair, to lie down and die, well, sleep anyway, was too strong. But my new human friend had gone up a ramp to a higher, brighter level. My new pack of canine friends had gone back to the sewer, to home, to what they knew and where they felt comfortable.

With callused paws I moved forward toward the ramp he used, pulling myself along, very slowly now, without much concern as to what might lay ahead. The hunger was gone, but I could barely move, and my fatigue was overwhelming. I wasn't really concerned about what might lay ahead because, as I've explained innumerable times, I could only fathom what was happening at the moment. (So how did I know that I've explained this innumerable times? Blame it on Dogspeak.) The past was past, as if it never happened. Yes, there was some echo of the man and the food, and the white pack of dogs was blurrily in there too, but it was all so vague. And don't even ask me about Francine and Reynaldo. You who know me know I'm only of this moment, so my whereabouts was confusing and strange and these ghost-like memories, the sense of what was normal, along with these surroundings didn't match up to my expectations. I wouldn't say I wanted to whimper or feel sad, but I was on the verge. . .of thinking. I'm talking about real thought, like a strategy to change my awful circumstance, something along those lines. And this thinking was not good, it was dangerous because I had lost my train of thought. My train of thought was: follow man, get him to remove wheelchair, me lie down and sleep. Simple, but that succession of thought just went out the window when I started "thinking", resulting in my completely passing by the man's ramp and traveling deeper into the building where that fabulous food table was.

Stage Fright

I'd come to an impasse. The food table was now far behind, my dark protector, and my bizarre pack friends, were even farther away, in distance and in memory. Confronted by a crossroads consisting of two ramps, my immediate focus was on sniffing out a direction, do I go left or right. My nose was not helping at all because both ramps smelled the same. As for texture, they were both easy to maneuver with my wheelchair. So, the only difference between the two came from my ears. There was heavy stomping and music from the left side. I was a little afraid of this noise but I thought it was human in origin and could lead to the end of this dark ordeal.

I turned left and trotted, yes, I actually trotted up the left ramp, even though my right paw was so raw. But, I was excited. I was anticipating something positive. What? I didn't know, but it was leading me forward to the music and the stomping and the shaking floor. It was scary, I do admit, but day after night after day of the same old cement walkway, (that's at least two breakfasts and two dinners), the rat battles, meeting the strange pack of dogs, not to mention the man, it was time to experience something that might possibly be normal.

So forward I went toward the music, which was now louder than the stomping. This ramp was taking me to a large doorway with what appeared to be daylight pouring out of it. If I went through the door, with all of that music and stomping, would it lead to the street? It was definitely loud enough, and bright enough, to be the street. This was what I'd been hoping for. This

was a dream come true. Were Francine and Reynaldo, not to mention food, water, and sleep, right around the corner?

At that moment I was two Corgi lengths away from the door. Coming from such complete darkness, the light was painfully bright, but that wasn't going to stop me.

I trotted through the door and on to the floor of a huge room full of people wearing, from a dog's point of view, strange clothing. This was not the street. This was not a dream come true. In this room, with its vast ceiling covered with iron walkways and a million lights of varying colors, the people were executing a syncopated series of movements seemingly stimulated by the music. This disturbing scene could only be described as controlled chaos. The street must have been across this room.

Within this noisy, chaotic forest of feet and ankles were a man and a woman who swayed side to side as opposed to leaping. All around them the males threw the females into the air. When the women were air-borne, the men leapt up to catch them, creating what appeared to be more floor space for me to walk on. Floor space that appeared and then disappeared so quickly that my sense of what my next step should've been, the logic of forward movement for a dog, was not working. The situation had become life threatening because when the men's feet hit the floor they were carrying the women, causing a force so strong that the floorboards bent a little each time.

Yet I persisted no matter what the danger. Actually, the concept of danger didn't enter into my thinking at all. I was just

plain scared, my body shaking uncontrollably and my brain addled. I persisted because I knew I had to get to the other side, not for access to the street, but just to survive.

There was so much information I had to sort out simply to take one step forward. Each time the dancer's feet hit the floor, the music produced an extra loud crashing sound that was murder on my ears and caused me to shudder. And then to top it all off, the music completely stopped momentarily then started up again at full volume.

I had begun to notice a structure or plan that might help me find a path to my goal. Since the men threw the women into the air and then caught them when the music signaled them to do so, I began to count on the music to give me the cue as to when to move forward or stop, whichever the case may be (I think it

should be noted that for me to figure this out was utter genius. No other dog could do this). There was a definite pattern made by their precise positions on the floor, with spaces wider than my wheelchair all the way to the other side of the room. So there was at least that. It was enough to give me hope, to keep moving and not to just stop where I was, which was nearly in the middle.

And on the other side was another door, maybe to the street.

That portal was dark, and there were people watching the leaping men and women. My goal was to get to the other side of the room using these spaces without being under one of the men when he came crashing down to the floor. I'd decided that it would definitely be to my benefit to be noticed.

It was so strange being among so many people and yet, not one had noticed me. I'm usually the center of any gathering of people. This only added to my confusion. I thought I'd better bark. "Barooof, barooof" I barked, to no avail. I tried twice more but my timing was way off. My statement was completely swallowed up by the music, so I abandoned barking and resumed moving across the floor.

I moved slowly between the men. I had to remember that when they jumped up and left a vacancy on the floor, the newly created space was temporary, because they came down immediately. This is what was called a concept and I was simply not conceptual in the least. A space is a space and it should have been forever, so I really didn't expect a falling foot to fill it up. I was having a hard time with this and the jumping was now at a furious pace with the music building in volume and intensity.

Utilizing extreme care and an uncharacteristic focus, I had covered about two-thirds of the floor when I noticed that to my right there were rows and rows of seated people looking straight at me. The "room" was much larger than I'd imagined. And over these people was a huge chandelier, only slightly emitting light but ever so noticeable. How calm they appeared in contrast to all of these jumping people. I could see them pointing to what I hoped was me. I wanted to be noticed, and maybe even picked up and taken away, or at least freed from my wheels. The jumpers, on the other hand, hadn't the slightest idea I was there. The men were busy catching the women.

While looking to my right and noticing all of these additional, calm, seated people, I had taken my attention off my, until now, carefully plotted course to the other side and noticed, in the dark portal the man, my new friend from the sewer, who fed us so well, and who seemed to genuinely love all of us, being placed on a gurney by people in white. The activity in that wing overwhelmed my concentration, and so, as you might expect, BOOM…YEEEELP! A man had landed directly on my raw and tired right front paw.

The pain was unbearable. I couldn't believe what I was feeling. My entire body had become so weak that I laid my head down on the floor, paws out in front, the right one bleeding and throbbing, my posterior in the air, suspended in the wheelchair, and my eyes tearing up to the point of near blindness.

My yelp, my scream, occurred right when the music paused for split second, or in human speak, a whole rest. And because of the yelp, my calm onlookers stood up and uttered a collective gasp that clouded the entire room. This time the music didn't resume and the man who crushed my paw was staring at me in disbelief with his hands on his face. The other people on the floor started to gather around. Apparently they were through with jumping and now had time to notice me. My operatic yelp had now deflated itself to a whimper.

The women who were being thrown about by the men just seconds before, were now pushing the men out of the way to see what had happened. One of them bent down and I could see she was upset. I was still in unbearable pain and if I could've writhed, I would have, but the wheelchair held me back from such comforting behavior.

I saw this woman begin to touch my paw and I thought, NO! And I yelped again, before she even touched it. I almost bit her! This was all happening in seconds, I'm sure, and no one could quite figure out what had just happened, me included. No one was even talking yet. Or if they were they were whispering, and not in English. Of course I didn't know it, but these people could never have imagined that a Corgi, or any dog for that matter, would be part of their dance. And then I suppose my wheelchair added another dimension to the whole experience.

So, while we were all taking in the situation, again, this in a matter of seconds, two woman were coming to the stage from the audience. The dancers were beginning to talk a little and a ballerina was on the floor petting me and saying soothing (but strange) words in my ears. I still looked straight ahead, whimpering, with my chin on the floor and my paws splayed out in my famous Y formation, almost 90 degrees from my shoulders.

At the same time, the people in white were wheeling my old friend, who had lifted his head a bit to see why the performance had stopped, away. When he saw me a wave of recognition crossed his misshapen face. He even managed a look of concern, which was quite remarkable considering his condition. He kept looking until they wheeled him around a corner and out of the building. None of my group noticed him or any of the commotion in that wing. They had their own drama to deal with here.

The dancers started to move away from me to make a path for someone. They were whispering "it's Brigitte Bardot, it's Brigitte Bardot!" Why they weren't whispering "it's Winnie" I'll never know but apparently this women was important to them. When she had reached me she sat on the floor and tried to offer some comfort. Another woman, a friend from home, Paulette Espin, appeared at the same time. Madame Bardot, who was petting me, sat back to give Paulette easier access. Paulette explained who she was, who I was, and that she would take care of me. Who would have thought that Francine and Reynaldo's good friend would be in the audience that night. And what luck that Madame Bardot was also there. Her love of animals was going to come in very handy.

I laid there unmoving and everyone was either kneeling or standing, all crowding around, watching me, Paulette, and Madame Bardot, who was petting me and letting her blond locks flow over my face. Although Madame Bardot's electrical radiations felt as comforting as Francine's would have had she been there, I was not able to register anything other than pain at this point, but I did notice a tear fall from Madame Bardot's eye onto my nose.

Paulette was taking charge. Her first act of kindness was to free me from my wheels. You have no idea what this meant to me. I instantly rolled over onto my unbitten side and just luxuriated in being off of my feet for the first time in ages. She explained to those in close proximity that I was Winnie—of The Winnie Chronicles fame. At that the dancers abandoned their interest in Madame Bardot and gathered a little closer to this bedraggled canine celebrity.

Madame Bardot looked relieved to have the spotlight deflected from her and took out her iPhone to make arrangements for some much needed doctoring with the vet she used in Paris. She asked Paulette about my spine and if I suffered any other maladies and said that her vet would be here shortly.

While they were speaking, I felt progressively sicker and suddenly everything got darker. As Paulette held my head, Madame Bardot touched my paw and then, poof! I was out.

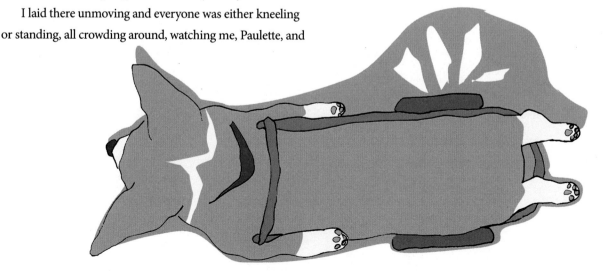

Paulette and Brigitte

After some intense doctoring by the vet, my paw was "set" in a soft, white cast that curiously matched my uncast paw, my "white stockings" as Madame Bardot called them.

The rat's dinner (my haunch) was stitched and bandaged and in general, I was cleaned up to a very high standard. Though it was tender, my paw was intact, nothing broken and, actually not too painful to walk on. I was back to "wheelchair" status and was able to function as I normally did, albeit much more slowly. Paulette and Madame Bardot exchanged numbers and Paulette was to call her if she needed anything, "anything at all, ma cherie". She stayed throughout the entire ordeal and even said not to worry about the bill.

Paulette and I traveled by taxi back to her hotel. It was a tense situation at the hotel desk because pets weren't allowed. Paulette explained my situation but the manager would not budge. The hotel had a strict no pet policy. So Paulette called Madame Bardot, who immediately asked to speak to the manager. After some very loud conversation on the phone end and much, "Oui, Madame Bardot," on the manager's end. We had our room.

Our new best friend, the manager, and two bellmen escorted us to our fifth floor room to retrieve Paulette's luggage and belongings so that we could move to our new digs on the sixth floor – a one-bedroom suite – that the management thought we would be most comfortable in. Paulette declined their offer because of the astronomical expense of such grand surroundings,

but the manager said not to worry, everything had been taken care of. He didn't explain further, but Paulette assumed Madame Bardot had something to do with it.

Once settled in, Paulette reflected on the bizarre events of her last few hours in Paris. She had wanted a relaxing night out at the ballet, a soothing distraction. She had been worrying about Francine and Reynaldo since they hadn't shown up at their hotel, or contacted her to say why. (I actually wanted the exact same thing.) And then this. Me. On stage at the Paris Opera in the performance she was, by incredible coincidence, attending. It was too perplexing. What was going on?

She had contacted the TV show where Reynaldo and Francine were to appear, but they had no information and were as worried as Paulette about their whereabouts. She called the police but they said that to file a *rapport de personne disparue*, a missing persons report, she would need some proof of foul play, otherwise it was something in which the French police would not get involved. Over twenty four hours had past, and she had called Isami Noguchi who was dog sitting Parsi, Paulette's pet wolf, several times for any word, any news that may have come his way, or if he had heard from David Northridge or Dr. Cougar, two friends who would likely be contacted if something were amiss. But no word had come their way.

Ironically, with just one Dogspeak retrieval I could shed light on everything she wanted to know, but Lord Northridge's lab was in Delaware, so that was out of the question. I was just glad to

be with Paulette in a room that had carpeted floors, water, and a place to fall over and sleep without having rats eat me. I'll bet Paulette was thinking the exact same thing. Not the falling over and rat eating part but the Dogspeak retrieval part.

At least, she thought, she'd find out how Francine, Reynaldo and I got separated.

49

Alan Tells Alain a Story

Propped up in my hospital bed staring out the window, I was drifting in and out of wakefulness thinking of what had happened to me and, more importantly, what would happen to me. But these thoughts were just too overwhelming for my present state of mind so I broke that line of thought by conjuring up my four legged buddies down in the sewer. I'd grown to love and miss those dogs and thought "wouldn't it be nice if they were all snuggled up on the bed with me". Then I thought about how big they were and how they'd step all over me. I'd probably end up back in the ER to re-do my stitching. So I gave up and went back to moping.

I kept going over the sequence of events right after I was hit, especially how strangely I'd acted, even for me. I knew I would have some explaining to do. People would want to know why I ran away, and why I waited so long to get help. I spent maybe a good twenty-four hours bumbling around down there with the gang, and when I surfaced people didn't ask if I was all right, which you couldn't really ask in good conscience because I was red from head to toe with blood, they asked "why did you leave?" I couldn't tell them that I was too embarrassed, mortified, and mostly, too vain to stay. I told them a partial truth instead, that I was confused. But I knew full well why I ran away and I was a little ashamed.

When I emerged backstage, it was as if Elvis had come back from the dead. People stood there with their mouths open. Everyone stopped what they were doing and looked at me with the awe that I had always wanted—from my dancing. But this was an awe of a different color, and I hated it.

When I say "emerged", I really mean crawled. I crawled to the feet of Kristal, our lighting director, and grabbed her ankle. She screamed! Then she saw me and knelt down to help. She started crying and said, "Alain, where did you go? What happened?" She, of course, knew what happened. One of her damn lights fell on me and ruined my life. But that wasn't what she meant. She, and everyone, wanted to know where I went after "the event" and what did I do for those twenty-four hours before I came back for help. She said four members of the company went looking for me.

Things moved rather quickly after that. Someone called for an ambulance. People gathered around and someone covered me with a blanket. Another gave me some water. And then I was lifted on to a gurney. The ambulance crew positioned me on my good side with my face staring out at the stage. I had a nice view of this evening's performance, a tarantella of sorts, that I was so glad not to be a part of.

As they attached an I.V. drip to my arm, I watched the most bizarre spectacle I'd ever seen, and I don't mean that tarantella. I thought they'd given me some sort of drug, because I was watching that little corgi in the wheelchair from the sewer come toward me. She was looking straight at me. I knew she was a dream, but I was so happy to see her again. I started to choke up with emotion. Those dogs, what love. Seeing her little face, maybe a little worried looking, but cute just the same was a nice sendoff

for my trip through the streets of Paris to this hospital bed.

This massive place, Hopital de l'Hotel-Dieu was actually quite homey. There were flowers everywhere in my (paid for by the ballet) private room, a nice chair for visitors to visit in, and a new TV to while away the hours. I had I.V.s and bandages galore. My pain was gone for the moment, but I couldn't trust that and with every little twinge I felt that something devistatingly painful was about to happen. The doctor described to me the various traumas my body had endured. My face had multiple lacerations and a broken cheekbone. My leg was deeply cut, but it was a cut that only grazed my thigh muscle and he saw no reason for me to give up dancing. I teared up at that. It was just too good to be true.

"Think of this as a medium intensity automobile crash, without the whiplash. Your face is going to heal. There will be some scarring and you can decide if you want to have cosmetic surgery down the road when we see how things are going. Your cheekbone is going to cause you some discomfort and we'll give you something for that, as will the leg, for that matter. For now, all you have to do is rest, build up your blood supply, and try to eat as much as possible," he said as he put my chart back on the footboard of my bed. "Don't worry Monsieur Picard. Worrying will take away your healing energy." He smiled at me and left the room. Easy for him to say. Worrying is my middle name.

People came, and people went, leaving kind words and

more flowers. I like flowers. I like them in gardens or maybe as a decorative accent in a stylish restaurant, but in a hospital room? What purpose did they serve? I know. I know. I'm not stupid, just cranky. I know the flowers helped the visitors get through the ordeal of visiting someone who was nothing more than a taciturn pile of flesh.

It was interesting just who did come to visit me. First through the door was our union rep, Sigmond Froun. What a surprise! Of course the union would want to know everything about the accident. Unfortunately, I was too spaced to give him anything worthwhile. There was nothing to tell. Everyone there saw what happened, and from a much better vantage point than I did.

About a third of my fellow dancers dropped by to wish me well and cheer me up. And their visits did cheer me up. I had no idea that anyone really cared. It made me feel so good. Then there was Sylvie Aubert, the director of the Ballet, my boss. She was in tears. I'd never seen her in tears. I almost sobbed right along with her. She assured me that I still had my job, and most importantly, my position. My mood did elevate at that news. And then came Alan Placard, yes Alan Placard, and I'm Alain Picard. I know, I know. Always a source of confusion. I was sincerely glad to see him. Alan was the only person I was remotely close to. He was one of those souls who could size people up upon meeting them. He was very good at that. He had my number: don't get too close but keep me interested. He always had a good story to tell. He was clever enough to bring a box of really special chocolates from the shop below his apartment instead of flowers. I appreciated the sentiment and would look forward to gorging on them when I was able to chew properly. But most importantly he told me about what happened at tonight's performance.

"Alain, you won't believe this. A corgi, you know, a dog like Queen Elizabeth's dogs, well this little corgi is in a wheelchair, can you believe this? And goes from stage right to center stage precisely in the middle of the performance precisely at the part where we're throwing the ballerinas up and catching them. Oh, I do not like this choreographer! Anyway, it was amazing. Then, and you can imagine how much danger she was in, Juan came down on her front paw. I mean, this had to happen. Poor little thing. She literally screamed bloody murder right when the whole rest happened in the music. Dead silence and then eeeeeech! So loud! We all looked down and saw her. We just stopped and stared. Juan was horrified. The audience gasped. Where did this little dog come from? And you know who was in the audience? Brigitte Bardot, the actress, and she came up on stage to somehow help the corgi, whose name is Winnie. Who turns out to be famous in her own right, from *The Winnie Chronicles*. No one can figure out where she came from. Quelle bizarre!"

Alain sat up a little straighter. He turned his head a bit so he could look out the window and then said, "I can tell you. I know where she came from."

"Quoi? No really. You do? You've got to be kidding."

"No, no. I mean it. She was with me for a good portion of my sewer journey. So were four other dogs. How she got down there I'll never figure out. Especially with her wheelchair." Alain said.

"Oh? Well, the women who took her, who was with Brigitte Bardot, said something about how Winnie's parents were missing. Maybe they're down there too. That could be how she ended up in the sewer. I think you should try to contact her. I'll get her name for you, Alain."

"D'accord. Oui, I should talk to her. I'd be happy to help. I don't have any information about the dog's owners, but I can tell her where I first saw Winnie. They could have gone on the sewer tour and got lost I suppose. But that doesn't make sense because they wouldn't take their dog with them. I'm sure dogs aren't legally allowed. Anyway, yeah, I'll talk to her." I said.

Love and War

At the junction of tunnels 14A and 14B, which lies under the border of the 9th and the 18th arrondissements, the neighborhood known as Pigalle, and almost directly under Le Theatre du Grand-Guignol on rue Chaptal, the long vacant and derelict theater in which horror plays were performed beginning in the late 1800's, was a wide staging and storage area for maintenance equipment known as A9/18. This area took the shape of a large, arched, brick room with a roaring river, the sewer's widest, running along its side. And in this room resided, along with various pieces of large equipment, the cousins.

The cousins, my first cousins, were a pack led by the smallest of what were incredibly large canines. Led by a female so fierce and foreboding that we had made sure that our "den", hidden away in what you might call a large closet, was located a safe distance — determined by smell — from A9/18.

This smallest of the cousins, whom we surmised was black or dark brown because our eyes could only sense her outline, had this reputation of fierceness as a result of a violent incident we witnessed.

When we were very young and little and new to this whole wonderful world, one of us, a now forgotten brother, (buried in our brains, but brought to the surface by this Dogspeak retrieval), was caught and devoured by her in front of all of us, including mother, who fought valiantly and sustained many wounds to no avail, as that brother ceased to exist within two or three minutes.

This was a life lesson. And though we were all born with survival instincts, none had come into play until those few, violent, bloody moments occupied our very beings, all of our senses, and all of our thoughts for many a moment afterward.

Then, as if by magic, and so typical of our canine brains, the life lesson faded, or I should say transformed, from an experience to a memory and then to a particle among many in our skill set of instincts designed to guide us, working in the background, always ready to pop up whenever this fierce and mean cousin was near. And now our once safe closet was under siege by the maintenance men who apparently needed to use rooms next to, and adjacent, our humble abode. This new activity had forced us to move into No-Dogsland, A9/18.

A9/18, known to us as a place to be avoided, not only because of the cousins, but lately because of human activity consisting of yelling and violent sounding behavior coming from one of the rooms leading off of A9/18, became — out of necessity — a temporary (and nerve wracking) safe haven for the four of us, a place a little less dangerous than our closet of a home with men milling about. Or at least that was the plan.

Another reason for our uprooting was the amount of non-maintenance men exploring our domain. We were being chased up and down the tunnels by people looking for the wounded man we had met earlier. We had heard them talking and calling out for him a little while after he fed us at that unforgettable food table. Our survival depended on all of us staying out of sight of anyone who ventured down here. True, we accepted the wounded man because we "saw" how he treated wheeldog, and we could also sense that he would not hurt us, but no other *human* had ever seen us.

So there we were, in the devil's territory, the lesser of three evils; people in the tunnels compounded by the cousins; multiplied by the yelling and violent sounds coming from one of the nearby rooms that made up the complex at A9/18. And it is in this place that what I, and my pack of brothers and sister believed to be true about our steadfastness and loyalty as a pack, wasn't.

The first thing we all noticed about our new surroundings was a certain, undeniable odor. It was coming from behind a large, mobile pumping machine parked next to the far wall from where we entered what I will now call "hell".

The next thing that caught our attention was how dangerously close we were to the human sounds coming from a room directly to our left. The room's door was slightly ajar, allowing a little light to pour into the hallway that separated our room from it. We were all on the most intense alert, ears up, tails out, and slightly crouched, ready to run or fight. And with our alert ears we heard, above the human noises, dog paws on the cement, and they weren't ours. All four "cousins" came out from behind the machine and were on their way over to us.

As they approached, that peculiar odor got stronger, an odor that I, and my two brothers, hadn't experienced before, an odor that instantly changed things among us, and not for the better, I'm afraid. We were now enemies. I don't mean my pack against the cousins, I mean my pack against itself, except, of course, my sister. Perhaps enemies wasn't right, maybe I should've said rivals. But no matter what you want to call it, truth be told, I should have sized up the situation and led us back to our old home with its own, more comfortable dangers. The odor had put

me in a non-leadership position, and though we needed to be a tight, focused fighting unit if we were to fend off the cousins, we were, instead a vicious danger to each other. And yet we also had to keep half an ear on the human activity as well since humans could be terribly dangerous. But such logic, such strategy, such loyalty, vanished as these molecules engulfed us, filled our eager noses with her "female" scent, her overwhelming power. We were under the spell of the cousins' leader.

Though none of us boys could see her very well, we could see a vague outline of her leaving the vicinity of the pumping machine. Her pack, the three "brothers," although who really knows what relationship these dogs have, approached us with a great deal of caution, and I must say I was surprised by this. They were a little ahead of her. At the same time my pack, except for my sister, were snarling and baring their teeth, AT ME! And I was doing the same thing to them and the cousins.

Within seconds, and displaying the most startling speed and agility, a large, white, male cousin reared up on his hind legs to do what? Punch me? It was a dumb move because I simply moved in and lacerated his stomach with my already snarling teeth. This action set off a biting frenzy among every dog in the room except the black female leader, who had a different agenda in mind.

The insanity we all experienced that afternoon was actually easily explained. We needed more cousins. Maybe she should have thought of that when she so cavalierly killed my little brother so many months ago. But leaving that aside, it was simply time to breed more cousins. And each of us males was meant to be the father of more cousins, at least in our minds. That was the logic behind it all, but the reality was just awful. My brothers were biting me, and each other, more than the attacking cousins were. And the racket we were making was echoing up and down the sewers. The ever-present sounds from the humans in the

room stopped. And then, during our carnage, a human came out of the room, very slowly and cautiously, to find the source of this powerful, angry noise.

The presence of the human was a game changer. My brother, who was skillfully attacking me, undid his teeth from my back and leapt onto the human when he showed his face, which is exactly where my brother bit him. I released the cousin I was biting and charged his leader. Instinct told me to put my teeth on hold for this next encounter. Instinct said "relieve this anxiety, end this obsession, make more cousins." And the great, fierce, leader of the cousins was receptive, my advance wasn't terminated with a death by tooth greeting, but with a "head forward and tail up" stance. This meant to me that I was right. I was right to approach her, I was right to leave the fight, and I was right to make more cousins.

And while we bonded, or I guess I should say, mated, the fight took a terrible turn. As both packs, the cousins and my brothers and sister were attacking a human, (male) a truly big noise rang out, and my sister fell over, lifeless and inert. I could do nothing as I was still in the mating process, but if I hadn't been doing what I was doing, I would have run from that sound. Soon, the echo of the sound died away and all five remaining fighting dogs mauled that man and one other who appeared from the room to within an inch of their lives, stopping only because three sewer maintenance workers had just arrived at the junction entrance. At the first sight

of these new humans, both packs backed away from the writhing mauled humans on the sewer floor and turned their attention on fresh prey. The maintenance men wisely sensed the danger they were in and realized that retreat was in order. They vanished in a flash from whence they came.

I had progressed through the mating process to its conclusion and was released by my most intimate archenemy. The aftermath, which might have been a time to reflect on the preceding, was cut short by the noise and violence all around. And my first instinct to fight her to her death instantly changed since I didn't want harm to come to the dog who would further my genes. She must have had the same instinct because she turned around and sniffed my face, without biting it off, and then trotted off to join her pack.

I was feeling good, although my brother had put a pretty deep hole in my back, and joined my pack as well. Both packs were now complete except for our motionless, inert sister. We sniffed her for a sign of life and found none. The writhing humans were no longer antagonistic to us, (as if they ever were), so we were through with them. We heard more humans in the room where these humans came from, but not wanting to expend any more energy we ventured back through the tunnel from where we came, all of us, both packs as one. All for one and one for all, momentarily, I don't doubt, but since A9/18 was now forever off limits, the search for a new den, or dens, had begun.

Is That Winnie?

Francine and Reynaldo were miserable. Reynaldo kept going in and out of consciousness and Francine kept going from worry to panic. She was most worried about Reynaldo. Then she'd switch to worrying about Winnie. Then she worried about what these two idiots would do to them.

She knew she had to get Reynaldo to a hospital, fast. The men who held them were thinking the same thing, but the whole mood of the abduction changed after the older man got that phone call. He didn't exhibit that same swagger as he did when they were first forced down here. And the younger one seemed very distraught. They'd stopped talking and she and Reynaldo were left alone. The only contact for the last few hours had been to ask permission to use the space outside the kidnap room to go to the bathroom. There were no facilities down there. Luckily, the younger one helped Francine with Reynaldo when he needed to go. But other than that, they just laid or sat on the cots that were set up in the room.

"I'm going to feed Reynaldo," said Francine to Laurent.

"Good. Go ahead," he replied.

"Have you thought any more about getting him out of here and to a hospital?" she asked as she opened a box of crackers. Gilles was cutting up some cheese and sausage and laying them out quite artfully on a paper plate.

"You can have some of this," he said.

"Thanks. I don't know if I can get Reynaldo to eat. I've been thinking. You could take him to the front of a hospital and just leave him. Don't you think? Just leave him out front and someone would take it from there. You'd never be seen," she said this in a straightforward way. Sort of conversational in tone so that they would see the simplicity of her plan and not notice from where it was coming.

"Yeah, yeah. I'm thinking about it," said Laurent. "I want to, but there's a problem. He'd have to go in a taxi. The driver would see me. I couldn't hide my face from the guy, so that wouldn't work." He made a cracker sandwich out of some sausage and cheese and took a bite.

"OK. That makes sense." Francine was adopting the tone of a fellow conspirator, solving the problem at hand. "How about this. We write a note, like 'My name is Reynaldo and I suffer from a neurological disorder. If you find me please take me to the nearest emergency room. Thank you.' And pin it to his jacket. You just lead him out of here and over to a busy street and take him into a store and then leave. If you wear your hoodie, cap and sunglasses you won't be recognized."

"It's still to chancey. I'd get recognized," said Laurent.

"No you wouldn't. There's so many young guys walking around with that look. You're not going to stand out." She was starting to lose her calm, starting to raise her voice.

"I wouldn't use Reynaldo on the note. Some other name, or no name," he said matter of factly. It seemed he was warming to the idea.

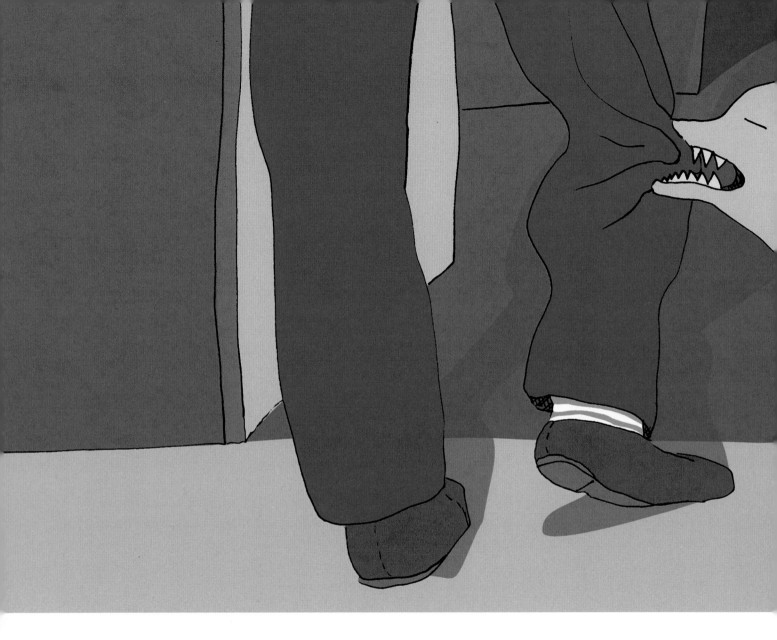

"OK. I agree. James. Just use James. It doesn't matter about the name, he just needs to go to the hospital and this is a way to do it. He could die. You understand that don't you?" She was raising her voice now, but she felt that they were on the way to the final negotiation on the method and procedure. Reynaldo could possibly be on his way in the next few minutes. And then there was a noise. It sounded like growling, lots of growling from many dogs.

"Is that Winnie? Winnie? Are you there?" she yelled.

The growling was escalating along with multiple toenail

clickings on the cement floor in the space outside the room where the stove was.

"Go see," said Laurent to Gilles. "Check it out. And bring me the Orangina I left out by the stove when you come back, please." He said 'please' in a way that indicated he was still angry with Gilles.

Gilles had been cutting more sausage when Laurent told him to find out what all the noise was. It was a scary noise and Gilles knew that Laurent was a little afraid. He'd always been weary of dogs, and this sounded like a whole bunch of them. Gilles got up from his cot, put down his plate and tucked his gun into the waistband of his jeans.

He walked out of the kidnap room and into the "cooking" room. The noise now consisted of out and out barking, snarling, and growling. In others words it sounded like a dogfight. He passed by the stove, saw Laurent's Orangina and then approached the door that Winnie had escaped through. He very slowly opened it wide enough for his head to peek through. It was very dark out there. He knew that this was a little entry way into one of the big rooms in the sewer system. That was where all of the noise was coming from. He slowly walked the few feet to the entrance to A9/18. He'd taken out his gun and cocked it.

As soon as he peaked around the doorway into that large chamber he felt searing pain in his face. He had been bitten and was continuing to be bitten by a very large and ferocious beast. Gilles' face was wet with blood and saliva. The dogs breath was otherworldly. He couldn't think, only react. He pulled the trigger. The gun went off. It didn't stop the biting, but he heard a squeal farther out in the room. Another dog joined in to aid Gille's attacker. This one was even bigger, stronger, and

he brought Gilles down to the floor while he screamed out, "Laurent, Laurent, help, help!"

Francine and Laurent could hear it all so clearly from where they were. When Laurent heard the shot he sprang up and ran out of the room. He didn't even hesitate even though he knew that Francine might try to escape. He heard Gilles screaming his name and he ran to the sound. When he emerged from the little entry way into the chamber where the savagery was coming from, he saw Gilles on the cement floor, bloody and unrecognizable. He wasn't moving but the dogs weren't done with him. They were in a ferocious frenzy, biting each other as well as poor Gilles. Laurent saw the gun next to Gilles arm and he went for it. But before he could take two steps toward it, three dogs jumped him and brought him to the floor, tearing at his body from head to toe. In a few minutes time Laurent was unconscious.

Francine knew it was now or never. They had never been this alone during their captivity, one or the other of their captors was always positioned by the door. Now was the time to move, and fast! She crept over to the door of the cooking room and found it empty. She told Reynaldo, "You've got to stand, Reynaldo! Try to stand up. We can leave now, but you have to stand up. Lean on me. Reynaldo!" she snapped, trying to wake him from his stupor. "Come on honey, we can go now." She had his arm over her shoulder and he was standing up. A true miracle! Francine had no idea how much time they had. She was beginning to panic. "Come on Reynaldo, you can do it. We can go home now," she said into his ear, whispering encouragement as they stumbled to the door. She picked up one of the flashlights that was always near the door, switched it on, and guided Reynaldo out of the dank and dark and into the daylight of Paris, France.

The Global News Today

If You've Got It We Want It

FRANCINE DUMONT ON LE GRAND JOURNAL DISCUSSES KIDNAPPING

By Daphne Shoeman

Francine Dumont, artist, illustrator, and owner of Winnie, the Corgi in the wheelchair and center-piece of *The Winnie Chronicles* appeared on the French television show *Le Grand Journal* last night on **Canal+**. The discussion was confined to the recent kidnapping of Ms. Dumont, her husband Reynaldo Dumont, and Winnie in the 18th arrondissement. The studio audience was absent and only the show's host, Antoine de Caunes, was present to interview Ms. Dumont one-on-one for this special segment.

Some of the more intimate questions dealt with the emotional state the Dumonts were experiencing during their captivity. Ms. Dumont said, "It was like a 24 hour migraine," and that both she and Mr. Dumont were so frightened all of the time because the kidnappers, one of whom was armed, were on the edge of sanitiy, and not entirely sure of what they should to do with them. The striking of Mr. Dumont during their initial kidnapping caused him to drift in and out of consciousness, and he is now being held for observation at Hôpital de l'Hotel-Dieu.

The kidnappers, Laurent and Gilles Boucher, were complete novices, new to the world of violent crime. Their aunt, Marie-Christine Boucher, whose occupation is taxi driver, instigated the kidnapping as a way to help her nephews out of a financial jam caused by a drug deal gone wrong. Ms. Dumont went on to describe the lack of sanitary facilities

"even though we were actually in the sewer," and the lack of food, causing both she and her husband to feel progressively weaker toward the end of their ordeal. Ms Dumont said," They had stacks and stacks of canned food and water, but the kidnappers were so distracted and scared, they never got around to actually feeding Reynaldo and me until the end, when we had cheese and crackers."

When asked why they were kidnapped, Ms. Dumont said the kidnappers wouldn't speak to them, other than ordering them around, and never gave a clue as to what this was all about until we were very late in the game. "That was the truly awful thing about it. We imagine they assumed we had accumulated some wealth because of *The Winnie Chronicles*, but we only found out after our rescue that a ransom of 1,000,000 euros had been demanded. And overriding everything was that a few minutes after we were abducted and led down into the room where they held us, Winnie disappeared through a door out into the sewer system. We were sick with worry. She was without food, her main source of joy for one thing. Only later, through a retrieval, did we find out food and Winnie had met up at one point. We also discovered the bizarre adventure she had while wondering around in the sewer. This could only happen to Winnie!"

Mr. de Caunes then asked if it was alright to ask about Mr. Dumont's head injury. Ms. Dumont answered that "Reynaldo was hit on his forehead straight away in the cab, before they herded us down into the sewer. He was bleeding pretty badly and was very unsteady on his feet. The doctors say that he suffered a concussion between mild and severe. Many times while we were down there he passed out. He only became alert and more like his old self when the dog packs started growling and barking in the room next to where we were imprisoned. He thought maybe Winnie was coming back."

In the last part of the interview, Mr. de Caunes asked Ms. Dumont what those

Winnie happy to be home.

last moments before the police arrived were like. "We had no idea that the tremendous racket the dogs were making meant that the end was near. I could tell from the sound that these were very large dogs and that they were fighting to the death. But I only got a twinge of hope that maybe a change was coming when one of our captors (Gilles Boucher) ventured into the fray out of curiosity. I was thinking at the time, what a fool, but he had his gun and I heard him use it. Then I heard him scream. I didn't dare get up to go near that door, since the other man (Laurent Boucher) was still watching us, but then after a very tense, short time, he decided he'd better see why Gilles screamed. As soon as he stepped out into that room he let out a yell I'll never forget. The noise, the barking and yelping went on for a bit then abruptly stopped.

That's when I got up off of the cot and peaked into that room. I immediately knew it was over. I got Reynaldo to his feet and we headed for our freedom.

When asked to describe what she saw, Ms. Dumont explained that she only looked into the room next to the kidnap room. There was a small entryway into the room with the dogs that she did not look into. Police reports stated that both kidnappers were barely alive, after having been mauled over ninety percent of their bodies. The doctors who treated them predict they will spend the remainder of their lives horribly disfigured and in wheelchairs. Their trials are slated for next fall. Their aunt, Marie-Christine Boucher suffered two broken legs as the result of an automobile crash she experienced while speaking on her cellphone. Her trial will begin in a month.

The Dumonts returned to Wilmington Delaware, USA last Friday. Mr. Dumont has partially recovered from his injury and is working with Winnie on retrieving more details of her experiences in the sewer. His partner at *Dogspeak*, Lord David Northridge, is in Normandy getting retrievals from the albino sewer dogs who now reside at Brigitte Bardot's animal shelter.

Francine Dumont has resumed her work as an artist.

Epilogue

The journey back to Wilmington from Paris was blissfully uneventful. Winnie enjoyed many of the same pleasures she had experienced on her way to Paris. Still wounded and in pain, Winnie did not let that get in the way of enjoying the second meal of fish in her lifetime.

Reynaldo's head wound was healing nicely on the surface, but causing some memory problems and headaches. His doctor is watching him closely.

And after a week of settling in at home, Francine began a long overdue search for a companion for Winnie on the internet. Within minutes of scrolling through a couple of rescues, she spotted a tri-color Corgi with a wounded, half-closed eye named Bridget and she knew immediately she had found Winnie's new partner in crime.

Back in Paris, after a complete police investigation into the kidnapping and the realization that the pack of dogs that led to its discovery were, in fact, quite vicious, a city wide call for the eradication of the packs of dogs living in the sewers of Paris was gaining steam until the French actress and animal rights activist Brigitte Bardot stepped in and rescued all seven of them. The dogs were officially adopted by her and kept at her Mare Auzou Refuge in Normandy, France, where they were socialized to some degree.

The leader of the larger pack gave birth to five puppies, two boys and three girls, all with blue eyes, dark brown fur, and perfect vision.

P.S.: We wish to thank Madame Bardot for allowing access (for *Dogspeak* retrievals) to the sewer pack dogs. Their memories of the events in the sewer were of immeasurable help in piecing the events of this story together.

Dogspeak 2.0

Good heavens how versions fly! We are all the way up to Dogspeak version 2.0. Dogspeak is the animal (excepting parrots) mind retrieval program invented by Lord David Northridge, with a little help from Reynaldo Dumont, and is responsible for translating my thoughts into what you are reading now. I, Winnie, on the other hand, am still at Corgi version 1.0. I must say that I haven't changed a bit other than some puffiness around the eyes and a sprinkling of snout gray.

With this new version come many additional features such as the use of the metaphor, utilizing the digitized version of Lakeon and Jonston's Book: *Like a Metaphor*. The use of metaphor is uniquely human and has a tremendous influence on the human way of thinking. Their book, which categorizes metaphors and similes by subject matter, allows Reynaldo's interpretations of my retrievals to flow a little less awkwardly and is the sole reason why I seemingly perceive things in a light that mirrors your own experience. *Dogspeak* will even throw in a synecdoche now and then.

A brief note on the power of retrievals. As amazing as it is that a computer program can "read my thoughts", translate them into any human language and thereby allow humans to experience what an animal experiences, it can't create a dialect for each subject. For English translations (and all languages for that matter), *Dogspeak* is linked to and bound by proper grammar, rules of syntax, etc. You'll never find an animal with,

say, a Brooklyn accent or a Scottish brogue or incorrect grammar. It's purely thought translated with a tremendous amount of embellishment into language, period. If a retrieval subject is rough or gentle in nature, pure-bred or other, you'll just have to rely on its actions to clue you in.

And further, you might have seen a chart or read in a book a hierarchy of canine breed intelligence. Please believe me when I tell you that the listing of a breed's intelligence is based solely on the human point of view. When it comes to *dogo y dogo*, we are all equally smart. The ranking goes from 1 to 79 and some of you may know that the border collie is ranked number 1, we Corgis are ranked number 11. Number 79 is jealously held onto by the afghan hound. I've been friends with or done battle with, many a breed, (including "mixed"), and I've never encountered a dummy. *Dogspeak* retrievals prove this.

Another new feature is called RAM Brevity. Lord Northridge streamlined *Dogspeak* so that my stereotactic cap is plugged into a MacBook Pro instead of the shelves of computers he used to use. Now my retrievals can be downloaded on the run, as it were, if the need arises.

Noting the greatness of the invention of *Dogspeak*, the scientific community has awarded the coveted Howard Crosby Warren Medal of Scientific Achievement to Lord Northridge.

The third, and most important new feature is called "voice recall". It, simply put, lets my mind relay any conversation I have heard to *Dogspeak*, which then captures it verbatim and incorporates it into the flow of information that I, (or any mammalian subject) impart to you. When someone speaks, I hear it, memorize it, and relay it to Reynaldo through a retieval.

Yes, *Dogspeak* has come a long way. From Lord Northridge's early work on the visual perception of fish to what has all of the appearance of dogs speaking (though frustratingly, this is always a one way conversation), it is nothing short of a miracle, as am I.